If the Fai

She'll live ha

In these contemporary twists on classic fairy tales from Harlequin Romance, allow yourself to be swept away on a jet-set adventure where the modern-day heroine is the star of the story. The journey toward happy-ever-after may not be easy, but in a land far away, true love will *always* result in their dreams coming true—especially with a little help from Prince Charming!

Get lost in the magic of...

Their Fairy Tale India Escape
by Ruby Basu

Part of His Royal World
by Nina Singh

Cinderella's Billion-Dollar Invitation
by Michele Renae

Beauty and the Playboy Prince
by Justine Lewis

All available now!

Dear Reader,

Billionaires are the thing right now. I mean, millionaires are so last year, am I right? But having all that money can weigh on a person. It's gotta be a tough gig. (I'm only guessing.) So I wanted to explore a billionaire who was reluctant about all those dollar signs in his account. What kind of man would he be? And how would he move through life? And what kind of woman would fit into that world he navigates with caution? I love a man who knows what he wants and how to get it. But we all know the best men are enhanced by the presence of a woman who may not necessarily understand him but who is determined to do so. So while finding a man with all those billions may be a fairy tale, the fantasy is definitely worth it.

And speaking of fairy tales, wouldn't you love an evening out in a fabulous designer gown and on the arm of a handsome man who only has eyes for you? My heroine has difficulty accepting the good things in life, and so she needed a little nudge. I had fun exploring Wolf and Ivy's world. I think they are perfect for each other, and I hope you'll enjoy the story.

Michele

Cinderella's Billion-Dollar Invitation

Michele Renae

Recycling programs
for this product may
not exist in your area.

ISBN-13: 978-1-335-59655-0

Cinderella's Billion-Dollar Invitation

Copyright © 2024 by Michele Hauf

For questions and comments about the quality of this book, please contact us at CustomerService@Harlequin.com.

Harlequin Enterprises ULC
22 Adelaide St. West, 41st Floor
Toronto, Ontario M5H 4E3, Canada
www.Harlequin.com

Printed in U.S.A.

Michele Renae is the pseudonym for award-winning author Michele Hauf. She has published over ninety novels in historical, paranormal and contemporary romance and fantasy, as well as written action/adventure as Alex Archer. Instead of "writing what she knows," she prefers to write "what she would love to know and do" (and yes, that includes being a jewel thief and/or a brain surgeon).

You can email Michele at toastfaery@gmail.com.
Instagram: @MicheleHauf
Pinterest: @ToastFaery

Books by Michele Renae

Harlequin Romance

Cinderella's Second Chance in Paris
The CEO and the Single Dad
Parisian Escape with the Billionaire

Visit the Author Profile page
at Harlequin.com.

To all the backyard entomologists who love watching dragonflies, beetles, butterflies and other bugs. It's a fascinating world we all share!

CHAPTER ONE

THE CLATTER OF plastic on the worn wood desk-top prompted Wolf to shift his sight from the computer screen, effectively surfacing from his mental foray through the python computer code that occupied his early mornings. The director of operations of Concierge, his best friend Skyr Svedahl, stood on the other side of the desk, hands on his skinny hips, curly blond hair always falling over one eye.

Wolf plucked up the daily desk calendar Skyr had set down and shrugged. "What's this?"

"It's a challenge calendar," the man announced with declarative gestures.

Wolf crimped a brow. "You know this company does have an app for that?"

"Really?" Skyr mocked uncertainty. "A calendar, sure. But not with challenges for each day."

Wolf had created the Concierge app years earlier. It organized all apps on a person's phone into one central hub. Everything from your grocery order, dinner deliveries, gas mileage, texts, alerts for monthly payments, medical info, household appliance reminders, fertility cycles for women, workouts, and all things baby related. If a person had an app on their phone, it could be incorporated into Concierge in one way or another. It had gone viral in the first week of its release. Last year Concierge had hit the billion-dollar sales mark. And since, Wolf's life had not been the same.

"Maybe you need to add this particular calendar format to Concierge," Skyr said. "See." He peeled off the top page that featured yesterday's May date. His actions were demonstrative and over the top. A showman during company meetings, the guy knew how to get a point across. "This is how low-tech items work. You gently tear the page. Feel the paper. Read the page…"

Wolf leaned back in the ultra-comfy high-tech office chair that could give him a massage, measure his heart rate, and remind him to get up and move every twenty minutes. "Not funny, Svedahl. Is this your way of apologizing for leaving Concierge next week?"

Skyr shrugged. "You know I'm in love. I would follow Melanie to the ends of the world. And Sweden is my home."

Wolf had met Skyr seven years earlier at a tech conference in Stockholm. They'd bonded over shared interests in the future of decentral-ization and craft beer. "We can make this work remotely, you know."

"I know. But I'm happy, Wolf. Thanks to Concierge, I've earned more than enough to live comfortably. Now I want to make a family."

"Yes, yes." Wolf gestured dismissively. "The simple life."

He'd never reveal how he completely agreed with Skyr's decision to leave the corporate rat race behind and settle into a low-tech, much more relaxed life with a beautiful woman and the hopes of family glinting in his eyes. All that living-off-the-grid jazz. He just needed space! Yet Wolf's chances of finding a woman who could truly love him had dropped off the charts. In fact, that miserable statistic had been the catalyst to his current dating sabbatical.

"I'll miss you, buddy."

"We'll Zoom. But here." Skyr nudged the calendar closer to Wolf. "Each day issues a challenge to try something new or do a normal task differently. You need this. It'll get you out of your rut."

"I'm not in a rut."

Skyr wobbled his hand before him and winced. "You come into the office every morning at five. You code until ten. You head to the coffee shop to fill up on octane. Spend twenty minutes sitting in the shop ogling the barista with the ponytail—"

"I do not ogle her," Wolf protested. His surveillance of the bright-eyed barista was more subtle than that.

"She's cute. I've checked her out. You should go for it. But I know you won't, because you are scared."

"Just cautious of my privacy."

"I get it. The paparazzi. But back to your rut of a schedule. Business meetings until two when you have a late lunch delivered right to your desk. Then work until it's dark. Sleep. Rinse. Repeat."

Wolf winced. When Skyr listed his routine like that it did seem mechanical and, very well, like a rut. He'd never been so focused on the job, determined, moving as if on autopilot. Unconcerned about having a social life. And what had happened to his libido? It was still there, but the relentless paparazzi—and a million-dollar lawsuit—really knew how to cool a guy's sex drive. But while the Concierge app had gifted him the ease of not having to worry about money, it had bracketed his world down to a tightly confined diorama of rote actions and daily grind.

On the other hand, his dull routine did keep the paparazzi away. Make a move in a new direction? Those curious camera hounds lurked, drooling for a salacious lede. Much like his office mates who gossiped behind his back. Could a man exist without the world wanting to know his every move?

"For your information," he said, "I'm not scared of the barista. I'm just…"

Cautious about dating. Especially when he never seemed to attract a woman he could trust with his fragile heart. "This calendar is half used." Changing the subject was much easier than talking about his nonexistent dating life.

"Because I've been using it. It's what made me decide to quit."

"Well, in that case…" Wolf picked it up and made like he would dump it in the trash bin.

"Do it for me," Skyr said. "I know you trust my opinions. Together we've grown Concierge into a company at which people dream to work. And don't I always have your back in Halo?"

They didn't spend much time online gaming anymore, but true enough, Skyr was a man who always had his partner's back. Virtual or otherwise.

"That calendar will change your life."

Wolf grunted dismissively. Then set the calendar on the desk. For now.

"I've got my replacement narrowed down to two candidates," Skyr said. "I'll give you my choice by the afternoon. Before I make my grand exit, do you want me to quell the office rumor that women are avoiding dating you because you're maybe gay?"

"What?"

Skyr shrugged. "Kidding."

"I haven't dated since before Christmas. Do they still gossip about my terrible dating life behind my back?"

Skyr nodded. "Janice set up a betting pool on how long before you do date. And how much the resultant lawsuit will cost you. Sorry, man. You just have bad luck with women."

It wasn't him. Was it? Wolf felt sure it was all the hundreds of millions that had suddenly befallen him. His last dissatisfied girlfriend had taken him to court for emotional distress brought on by a quarter-million-dollar diamond ring!

Thus, a sabbatical from dating.

"You know why I don't date," Wolf muttered.

"According to Page Six, it's because you don't like getting sued. But I know you, man. That last one was crazy. Just because you gave her a ring she thought that meant you were going to marry her?"

"I said nothing about marriage when I gave it to her. It was just a bauble she saw in a jewelry store, and I wanted to make her happy." Wolf raked his fingers through his thick hair. Buying things for others was the easiest way to ensure he held a place in their lives. "Is it too much to ask for someone real?"

Skyr swept his hand in Vanna White fashion beside the calendar. "This will help."

"I seriously doubt that, but I'll take it off your hands just to keep from seeing more of your Vanna impersonation. We done here?"

"We are." Skyr gave him a salute and left the glass-walled office.

Wolf owned the entire building. He'd thought by choosing something in the Chelsea area, better known for being the center of the art world, away from the financial and the techie Flatiron districts, that would promote a calmer atmosphere for his work life. Concierge was his safe space.

Becoming a billionaire had made him a celebrity, and that had flipped his calm, quiet world upside down. He hadn't even known what Page Six was until he'd started dating models and actresses. Initially he'd thought he'd hit the jackpot. Poor kid from a small village in Germany, once scrawny, who wore thick glasses, always beat on by the bullies, grows up to create an app that the world couldn't get enough of, thus making him strangely attractive to some of the most beautiful women he'd ever laid eyes on.

But none of those women had been capable of *seeing* him. The real Wolfgang Zeigler still sometimes felt like that bullied boy with the thick glasses and had a penchant for avoiding crowds because he preferred to isolate himself in the wondrous world of computer code. Coding was what made him happy.

Wolf leaned back in the chair and closed his eyes. With the one friend he was always able to talk to leaving, would he now fall deeper into the apparent rut Skyr had said he was in?

He opened one eye and read the sentence on the calendar page for the day. Stupid.

With a sigh, he shook his head. Skyr knew him too well. Wolfgang Zeigler was not a man to resist a challenge.

"Your turn, Ivy." Estelle Clement replaced the bean hopper on the espresso machine and then swiped her hands down her apron that bore the But First… logo for the coffee shop she'd owned for fifteen years. "I gave you my list of items required to make the perfect man. What about yours?"

Estelle had watched *Practical Magic* last night—for about the fortieth time—and she'd told Ivy about her favorite scene where the young Owens sisters make a wish for their perfect man. Estelle's list included blue eyes, the ability to mambo at the drop of a hat, and various bodily expectations that Ivy could wholeheartedly get behind.

They had become good friends in the three weeks Ivy had been working the morning shift as a barista. She was thankful for Estelle's kindness and that they got along. Otherwise, this soul-sucking menial job would annihilate her will to live.

"The perfect man, eh?" Sliding a soft-bristled cleaning brush along the stainless-steel machine components, Ivy focused on getting into the crevices. "Well, he has to be smart. Give me a real conversation over texting, please."

"Hallelujah to that one. I am so over emojis and hashtags. My boyfriend is a physicist. He can talk me between the sheets with the theory of quantum physics any day."

"Wow. You are not easy. I like that." She and Estelle bumped fists. "What else? He has to be strong. I like a man who can pick me up and carry me away."

"Oh, so you're into fairy tales, eh?"

Ivy imagined a man carrying a woman up a long stretch of stairs. Without dropping her or knocking her head against a wall. Yeah, probably fairy-tale stuff.

"I guess I am. Though ixnay on the glass slippers. I'm not much for pulling glass shards from my soles. He's gotta be protective, too. That goes along with the sweeping-me-away part."

"So, you are definitely into muscles."

Was she? She'd never devised a list of attributes for the perfect man. This was just a game, right? Well, if there was one thing she did require in a man…

"And he has to believe in love," she declared as she set the cleaned portafilter on the mat beside the espresso machine. The sudden jab of an elbow into her rib made her chirp. "Ouch!"

"Shh." Estelle leaned in and whispered. "He's back! Don't look. You know he comes in every morning just to see you."

Ivy rolled her eyes. Then she managed a glance out the corner of her eye while maintaining her attention on her cleaning task. "It's just his routine."

He was back. Wolfgang Zeigler. The man who owned the art deco building in which the But First… coffee shop occupied the bottom floor, alongside a twenty-four-seven gym. Assorted businesses filled the ten floors above them, mostly office space. The top two floors were dedicated to Concierge. Zeigler was punctual, always arriving at ten o'clock. And his order never changed. Black coffee. Slice of chocolate chip cake. Estelle had filled Ivy in that he was the creator of the wildly famous Concierge app. And he was a billionaire. Apparently, though, since his dating life had taken a dive, the street had cleared of paparazzi. Something Estelle cheered because the photogs had a tendency to scare away the customers in their frenzy to snap a shot of Zeigler's every move.

Was that all it took nowadays to garner celebrity? A fat wallet? Ivy supposed being a billionaire did make one a celebrity, but she much preferred her celebs to display talents that lifted her mood. Like Lucille Ball or Michael Bublé. From the little she'd heard about Zeigler on the news, he was a savant when it came to programming. He had a reputation for dating gorgeous women. And then dumping them less than a month, or even a week, later. Celebrity rags called him the rogue billionaire.

But what Ivy saw when he strolled into the shop was a ruggedly handsome man with thick black hair and a black beard and moustache. He looked like a lumberjack who had been caught by a styling team, pomaded, groomed, and released back into the wild. His uniform was a white business shirt, the top two buttons undone to reveal a peek of black chest hair, and the cuffs were usually shoved to his elbows, not neatly rolled. His trousers were perfectly fitted, yet the way they stretched across his backside revealed the fact the man must work out. He was built and beefy. Yet curiously reserved.

That was the part about him that intrigued Ivy. For a man who must have the world at his grasp and had dated famous people, he was guarded, even a little shy. She'd always thought those in the limelight shone brightest when given attention, so his quiet demeanor fascinated her.

Alas, she was a simple barista. At least for the moment. Certainly not a stunning model or actress capable of capturing the sexy man's attention. Nor did she consider dating a celebrity a sane move. Of course, that didn't stop her from daydreaming about him. How else to make the day go by?

Lifting her shoulders and smoothing a hand to tuck in the loose strand of hair that had fallen from her ponytail, Ivy forced on her "I'm a retail worker and must be nice to customers" smile and turned to greet the man who occupied her daydreams.

"Good morning, Mr. Zeigler." Who was she kidding? Her smile was natural and oh so easy when directed at him.

He nodded. She'd never been a woman to fawn over a handsome face, but this man had some serious bedroom eyes and that beard looked so soft she wouldn't mind getting lost in it. And if that meant their lips had to collide? Do not send out the rescue crew.

"The usual?" she asked, fending off wandering thoughts of five-alarm fires and kisses.

"Black coffee," he said, "and…" As Ivy bent behind the counter to reach for his usual snack, she paused when he announced, "A slice of lemon cake. Please."

She snapped upright, peering over the glass display case at the man who had stuffed his hands in the front of his trouser pockets. "What?"

He nodded. "Lemon cake, please."

"But…"

He took a moment to study her expression then shrugged. "I know. Thought I'd change things up today. And…" he pulled a folded piece of paper from one of his pockets "…my calendar told me to do it."

Ivy narrowed her gaze onto the paper he held for her to read. It had today's date on a little desk-calendar-size note. The logo *Challenge Yourself* was flourished across the bottom. And the sentence printed in the center read: *Try a new-to-you food today.*

This billionaire who could have anything he desired—and anyone, for that matter—took directions from a corny desk calendar?

"Well, okay then." She pulled out a slice of the lemon cake, frosted with a tart lemon glaze, and set it on the counter. Black coffee in a small cup, no cover, she set beside it. "Good luck with your culinary adventure."

A smirk revealed his reluctance at the change. "I'll need it." And then he peered at her chest for a moment. "Thanks, Ivy."

"You're welcome, Mr. Zeigler," she managed in a calm tone while her insides burst into a festive dance.

He settled into his usual seat by the front window, attention on his phone, and took a sip.

Meanwhile, Ivy was jerked around behind the stock shelves by Estelle. The woman's gold hoops jangled madly as she clutched her fists in glee before her. "Did you hear that?"

She had heard that. "He ordered lemon instead of chocolate chip," Ivy whispered, not wanting any of the patrons to hear them.

"No!" Estelle whispered enthusiastically. "He called you Ivy."

"That is my name."

"Don't be smart with me. I can sense your insides jittering with glee. That man has never called you by name, or anyone else in the café. He likes you." Estelle fluttered her lashes. "And he does qualify for both the strong and smart items on your list."

"Whatever. I need to finish cleaning the espresso machine."

Ivy picked up the cleaning cloth and went back to work, and acknowledged her insides were indeed doing the gleeful dance Estelle had discerned. The man with the intense yet softly searching brown eyes had called her Ivy. That had been the most personal thing he'd said to her in the three weeks she'd been serving him daily.

Drifting back into the fantasy of a soft beard and hard, tight muscles, she dared a glance over the top of the machine. She caught Zeigler in the middle of a bite. That wince did not signal approval. She hadn't expected he'd like the tart lemon. He was more of a constant, comfortable chocolate chip guy.

Tossing aside the cleaning cloth, she slid a plate out from the display case and then wandered around to the dining area. "How's that lemon cake working for you, Mr. Zeigler?"

He offered her another of those brief but captivating smiles. "I think it requires a certain palate."

"It's a bit tart." She set the plate with a slice of chocolate chip cake on his table. "Trade?"

He pulled the plate to him. "Hell, yes."

Retrieving the lemon cake, she was about to leave him to himself when he touched her wrist. "Hang on. I'll get my card to pay for it."

"It's on me," she hastened. "Seriously, Mr.

Zeigler, you're our most consistent customer. Every day at exactly ten o'clock. I can set my watch by you."

He swiped a hand over his jaw and beard. "You think I'm in a rut, Ivy?"

The question was so out of the blue she could but mutter, "Uh…"

"I know I am. This calendar is supposed to make me think out of the box. Do things differently. Not a very good start, eh?"

He liked to try new things? She mentally added that to her list for the perfect man. Why not? It was her list; she could edit at her whim.

"You did give it a try," she offered. "There's something to be said for taking a chance, especially if lemons have caused you trauma in the past."

His laughter was deep and easy. Ivy wanted to lean forward and stroke his beard. Make contact with the larger-than-life man who lifted her weary spirits each morning she saw him.

"No citrus trauma," he said. "Though, now that I think about it, there was that one time me and a buddy robbed a lemonade stand."

"You did not!"

"I was seven. And I needed the change for some new shoes." This time his wince seemed to take him unawares and he straightened, shifting his body to a less easy posture. "Ancient history. Thank you for rescuing me from that sour yellow cake."

"No problem, Mr. Zeigler. See you tomorrow at the same time?"

He thought about it a moment. "Maybe I should surprise you with a different time?"

"Now that would be stepping out of a rut," she teased.

"Yes, it would." He lifted his coffee cup in a toast. "Here's to trying new things."

"Hear, hear!" Ivy called as she strolled back to the counter where a customer waited. While she filled the complicated latte order, her focus kept drifting to the man who devoured the cake.

Trying new things? And he'd called her by name. This day was already better than any of them had been since she'd had to suddenly move to New York to take care of her brother. She'd had to refuse an excellent job offer for a position in Switzerland and find something close to where her brother was staying, thus the coffee shop. These past weeks had been a challenge. But she wasn't complaining. That never got a person anywhere. Besides, she'd get a chance at her life after she ensured her brother was on the right path.

And now she had something to add to her *Things to Be Thankful For* list. He'd called her

Ivy. And had actually spoken a few sentences to her.

Nodding with satisfaction, she peeked around the espresso machine to watch as Zeigler left the shop. A rogue billionaire? To her, he was more like an exotic insect perched on the edge of a jungle leaf, just out of her reach. Where he should stay. A mental reminder that he was a celebrity and she didn't need that drama in her life prodded.

Yet she'd never been able to resist the allure of the rarest of the species. Continued observance was required.

CHAPTER TWO

ON TUESDAY, Mr. Zeigler ordered the usual, went to his usual table, pulled out his phone, and began his usual—whatever it was he usually did for the twenty minutes he sat there.

Standing behind the counter, still taken aback, Ivy glanced to the clock on the wall behind her. Nine fifty-five. He'd come in ten minutes early. Wonders did not cease!

Picking up the coffeepot, she decided to also switch things up. He never requested a refill. But her ability to resist curiosity was weak. And mental field notes on his rare species were a necessity.

Arriving by Zeigler's table, she held up the pot in offer. "Refill?"

The man's focus switched from phone screen to the pot and then to her. His mouth softened into a genuine smile. It made her core swirl with a sensual heat. "Sure."

She filled his cup without losing her gaze in

his deep brown eyes. A feat, actually. "What does today's calendar page demand of you?"

"An easy one." He dug out the folded page from his pocket and handed it to her.

She read the unfolded square. "'Take a five-minute cold shower at the beginning of every day.' Easy?" She mocked a shiver. "Don't tell me you already do that?"

"It's good for the circulation. And a bunch of other health stuff. You don't do cold showers?"

"I'm not big on shock. Especially at five in the morning. And I'm pretty sure my scream would be heard by the neighbors in the brownstone next door. I'll pass."

"It's exhilarating. Kind of like when I walk in the door to But First..."

"Oh? This dorky little café gives you a lift?"

He nodded with a shy bow of his head. Then a shrug. It was as if he'd reverted from a confident billionaire to a small kid right before her eyes. A kid who didn't know how to express his feelings but had accidentally blurted out a private detail. Or more likely, an adult man checking his personal boundaries.

"Glad to hear it," she said. "I'll see you tomorrow, Mr. Zeigler. Whenever time that may be."

The touch of his hand on her arm paused her. A sensuous heat moved from her wrist where his hand made contact with her bare skin and

MICHELE RENAE   27

wavered up to her shoulders then spilled to her
breasts. Such a visceral thrill! She was suddenly
glad she wore a dark T-shirt and the heavy can-
vas apron because her nipples peaked tightly. So
much for personal boundaries.

"My name is Wolfgang," he said. "Call me
Wolf?"

Her entire body swam in the ocean of desire
that his deep voice conjured. And if she looked
at him one moment longer she would definitely
fall into his eyes. Ivy rescued herself from an
embarrassing plunge. "Wolf. The guy who owns
the building, right?"

"I do. My office is on the top floor."

"That's Concierge," she said. "I have the app."

His smile was, curiously, much closer to a
smirk. "Most everyone does."

"It's a life changer."

"Really? For the good or the worse?" he asked.

An unexpected question from the creator of
the famous app.

"For the good, of course," she said. "Stream-
lines my life. Reminds me of things I need to remember. Collates all the assorted other apps into
one quick look in the morning. It's all good."

"Fair enough." He leaned back in the chair.
"But…it doesn't make you feel like you're in a
rut? I mean, the app does everything for you.

You don't even have to think about things. Your phone pings. You check it and respond."

"Are you suggesting a person *shouldn't* use your app?"

He shrugged. "Never. I've just been thinking differently lately."

"Because of your calendar. Well, I'm pretty sure five minutes under cold water isn't going to change a person's life."

"You'd be surprised, Ivy." He stood and gathered his coffee cup and tucked a twenty-dollar bill under the plate. His usual tip. "Thanks. And, uh, don't forget. It's Wolf."

"I could never for—uh, yep. Wolf." She waved as he strolled out of the café. Only when he was clear of the front windows did Ivy exhale and shake her head. "Oh, my God, I'm such an idiot. I almost said I could never forget you, Wolf. Yikes!"

And yet, he may never realize he was the one bright spot in her day.

On Wednesday, Wolf strolled into But First… around ten-thirty. He'd just finished a workout at the gym next door. Not his usual evening workout time, so his entrance had made the receptionist do a double take.

He'd only been following the pages a few days and, weirdly, his brain had started to hit him with questions before he did things. Can it be done a different way? Would changing a tried-and-true method or routine make him pay closer attention? Even the few paparazzi who lurked in the neighborhood had been taken off-guard with Wolf's mixing things up. And that was a kick!

He knew this sudden need to pay closer attention to the details wasn't because of some stupid calendar. Because he'd finally talked to the pretty barista. He'd spoken her name. A name he'd read on her nametag in his head every day he'd gone in for coffee. And by finally speaking it out loud, it was as if he'd released a clasp on that shy young boy inside him who was always unsure about talking to the pretty girl. Hell, he'd touched her wrist!

Wolf met all kinds of women, all the time, and in every situation. It always started out friendly, then moved to flirtation, then most of the time his libido charged in and they hooked up, sometimes even for a few weeks.

But because of his innate desire to trust and be loved, he'd been burned by those women. They always wanted something from the man who had been branded with the mark of billionaire. It felt like a red letter on his chest. The app, and the brand he was growing around Concierge, attracted money like a magnet. Pretty

damned crazy for a guy who had grown up in
the foster system and had never had a bed to call
his own until he'd rented his first apartment at
eighteen.

"Good morning, Mr.—er… Wolf."

Ivy's voice was dulcet. But with a solid firm
edge. When he thought about her—which he
did as he sat nursing his coffee, pretending to
skim his emails—it seemed as though she didn't
quite fit in this cozy coffee shop, brewing lattes
and skinny mochas. She carried herself tall and
proud. Her sleek brown ponytail was always
tight and neat. He sensed the coffee shop's tex-
tured gray walls and white marble counters
studded with neon lamps was not her natural
habitat. And he wanted to discover more about
her. Because really, he'd not developed a coffee
habit until a few weeks ago when he'd spied the
beautiful woman behind the espresso machine.
He hadn't missed a morning since.

"The usual?" she prompted him with a smile
that glittered from her bright blue eyes. Hex
code 74D4E7. He knew the chart programmers
used for colors like the back of his hand. When
he nodded, she gestured to the empty table by
the front window. "I'll bring it out to you."

Wolf turned to face his table. *His table?* Really? *Yep, you are in a rut.* Turning, he eyed the
table in the corner. Why not?

When Ivy arrived with coffee and a slice of chocolate chip cake, he thanked her. "I know," he offered, with a gesture to take in his new digs. "Mixing things up."

"The corner table. It is prime real estate. Just don't let your knees nudge up under the table."

"Why?"

"Gum," she said. "I don't get paid enough to do that dirty job."

"Thanks for the warning, Ivy." Her name felt like candy on his tongue. He wanted to have a real conversation with her, something that went beyond pleasantries. And today he had his chance. But it could only happen if he shoved aside the shy boy and put on his big boy cap.

Wolf pulled out the calendar page from a pocket and handed it to her.

"Okay, let's see what today brings," she said. "Take a walk in the middle of the day. So how did that go?"

"I'm not sure. I was going to ask when you get a break. Would you go on a walk with me, Ivy?"

"Me?"

She looked around. The café hummed with the sounds of the espresso machine. No one paid them mind.

Please don't say no...please don't say no.

"I...uh...well, I do get off at two."

That was a yes! "Great. Will you walk with

me? Just around the neighborhood. I promise I won't keep you long."

"I'd like that."

"It's a date then. Er, well, I mean, it's a…" He fidgeted with the calendar page. Dates were off-limits!

"I know what you mean. It's another challenge! I'm happy to help you with it. I'll see you in a few hours."

Another barista called for Ivy's help, so she swung around and back behind the counter. Wolf followed her walk. Tall, shoulders proudly back, sexy sway at the hips. She was one beautiful woman.

Not in the right place, though. He couldn't shake that feeling about her. Interesting.

And he had not a date with her—but a challenge.

Hmm, he didn't like the sound of that. However he labeled the walk, he would finally get to talk to the woman who had the power to stir him from his desk every morning to take a break.

There was something about Ivy he couldn't get enough of.

Wishing she had worn something prettier than a T-shirt and jeans, Ivy reminded herself she was not on a date with the sexiest man she'd ever served coffee to. This was just a challenge he was completing. And she was helping. That made it much easier for her heart to manage as well. She didn't have the emotional energy for a relationship right now, but friendships were always welcome.

So it didn't matter that her shirt advertised that *Bugs Are Beautiful*, or that there was a hole in her jeans just above her knee—usually covered by the work apron. The day was bright and warm, and the route he'd suggested took them down a quiet street that led them to a small park. A yoga class currently occupied most of the park, so they strolled around the area beneath pear trees that had recently bloomed. Spent white blossoms gently snowed down on them. It felt magical.

But Wolf seemed nervous. He'd only asked how long she'd lived in the city—about a month and a half—and what she liked about working at But First... Not much, but she did enjoy the conversations with customers.

"Spiders," he suddenly said. He smiled at her double-take and then made an expert toss of his cup, landing it in the garbage can.

"What?"

"I paged back to the previous day that my friend had left on the calendar just to read it. It said to reveal a fear to someone. I'm afraid of spiders."

"Oh, well, arachnophobia is shared by most. Personally, I love the furry little critters."

"I get that from your shirt. That's why I brought up spiders." A flower petal landed on his sleeve and he observed curiously before brushing it away. "What's beautiful about a hairy, eight-legged creature that crawls over your hair in the middle of the night and bites your legs?"

"They don't all bite. And really, if I were a spider I'd go immediately for your hair, too. Oh." Ivy bit her lower lip.

"Because it's a good place to hide?" he asked.

No, because it looked soft enough to nuzzle her face into. And it probably smelled like leather or steel or some manly scent that she wanted to inhale and get drunk on.

"Arachnids are attracted to dark, confined places." Whew! Way to make the save. "But not all insects stir dread in your heart, I hope?"

"Just spiders." They rounded a corner where the sunlight was no longer blocked by the tree canopy. Wolf pulled out a pair of sunglasses and put them on. "Tell me what you're afraid of?"

Fair enough. Anything to make this conversation last.

"Fears?" Never getting back the life she'd almost held in her hands? Watching her brother be decimated by a malicious disease? "I'm not a big fan of horror movies or serial killers. I don't watch a lot of TV, actually, because I don't like to put that sort of stuff into my brain."

"I agree. I can't remember when I last flicked on the screen. I have one in my penthouse, but I'm pretty sure the dust has grown so thick…"

"That spiders have moved in?" she teased.

"Don't say that!" With a laugh he paused and leaned against the wrought-iron fencing that corralled the park. "This little park is nice. There's so much concrete and tarmac in New York. It was a major adjustment after I moved here from Germany." He thumbed a couple more flower petals on his shirt sleeve then offered her a warm smile. "I can't remember when I last took a few minutes out of the day to shift my focus from coding and business."

She had read something about him being a coding savant. "So you're the coding genius behind the app? That's cool."

He pushed the glasses up to the top of his head. Ivy was thankful for the move; she liked looking into his eyes. "I love coding. It's like a second language to me. Maybe even my native language. I'm a geek. What can I say?"

The last time she had seen such a muscled, sexy geek was never. He certainly didn't fit the geek model. "Geekery is good. And there's nothing wrong with avoiding media and all the sensational images that suck away your soul. So

what do you do with your free time? That is, if
you have free time."

"That's just it. I work a lot." He blew out a
breath. "Doesn't really seem to move the scale
much either."

"How do you mean?"

"Like, is all this work improving my life?"

"I seem to recall reading that you earned a
bit of cash from the app."

He chuckled. "I did. But money doesn't make
a guy happy or move the scale."

She might argue differently. The medical
bills stacked on the table at home certainly
would, too. She and Ivan, her brother, had not
yet reached financial panic mode. But it would
arrive soon enough.

"I think I'm at an inflection point," he said.
"I'm standing in the middle. I can go one way.
The usual way. Keep doing what I'm doing,
making more money that I don't need, pushing
apps on the masses that they don't need, and
life goes on. Or…"

"Or?" She leaned against the fence beside
him, propping her hands on the iron rail behind
her. Standing so close to him, she could smell
his—well, it wasn't cologne. More like a sweet-
ness and spice. Was it his hair product? Whatever it was, she could almost taste it, it smelled

so good. Aphrodisiac pheromone attractor, she scribbled in her mental field notes.

"That's the thing. I'm not sure what the *or* is. What could I have if I wasn't so focused, so stuck in this rut that feels so deep I'm drowning?" He straightened abruptly, gesturing before him. "Sorry. That was... Too personal."

But an excellent addition to her notes.

"It's okay. I like talking to you, Wolf. And even though this is just a challenge to you, I appreciate the chance to get to know you better. You're an interesting man."

"I can say the same about you. Bugs, eh?"

She shrugged. No reason to reveal her purpose for the T-shirt. She was, after all, just another page on his calendar.

All of a sudden, a shower of white petals rained over their heads. Ivy tilted back her head and closed her eyes. She could have been enjoying nature, working outside right now had Ivan not called her two months earlier with his devastating news. She was not a woman who could maintain her sanity for long confined in a little shop, pressing coffee grounds for a living.

When Wolf took her hand with both his, and the warmth of his touch traveled like fire up her arm, she sucked in a breath.

"Thanks," he said. "This means more to me than you'll ever know. I mean, you took time out of your day to give me your attention. I appreciate you going along with my silly calendar page."

"Always happy to help a man of discernment."

He lifted a brow.

"The chocolate chip cake. It's amazing," she said.

He chuckled. "That it is. You've a petal on your lashes. Can I?"

She nodded. As he carefully plucked it away Ivy took in his determined brown gaze, the tip of his tongue as it slipped out of the corner of his mouth. And that hair. So touchable. But she didn't see any petals on him that would require a subtle brush.

"Thanks," she said shyly.

Who had she become? She wasn't shy or mincing. She'd dated some amazing men and most of them had been handsome, prone toward the scientific arts, and always quite kind. She knew how to talk to and relate to a man. Not that any of her lovers had ever stuck around for more than a few weeks. That was her choice. She'd always been focused on school.

But there was just something so…intimidating about Wolf. Not in a scary way. But rather, in a manner that warned if she was not cautious she might succumb to his pheromones and—

"Should we head back?" he asked.

Wrenched from the image of falling into the

man's arms, Ivy nodded. She didn't want the walk to end. And she was off from work. But she did need to get home to her brother. Back to reality. Observation of her knight in rugged armor would have to wait for another day.

At that moment a dragonfly fluttered before them and she held out her finger. The insect landed, flapped its wings, and settled there, content.

"Wow," Wolf said. "You have some kind of bug mojo." He peered closely at the insect and his breath on her hand made her imagine his breath elsewhere on her body.

Really, Ivy? *Yes.*

But whether or not to net this particular man perplexed her. Because she wasn't just the person who shared an interest in his calendar pages, but rather, she was the woman who wanted to peel back his shy armor and see if his insides were as interesting as his outsides. Yet, with caring for her brother, she hadn't the emotional headspace to open up to him and allow him into her life on a relationship term.

Did she? Or, more honestly, *dare* she?

CHAPTER THREE

ON THURSDAY, Wolf sat down at a table on the opposite side of But First…, near a bushy plant that he flicked aside so it wouldn't tickle his neck. Ivy brought him black coffee and chocolate chip cake, and then waited for him to reveal his next assignment.

He handed her the page as she said, "Ten-thirty today. How do you exist on such a wild and crazy schedule?"

He initially took that as a dig but then realized she was joking with him. The last time he had been able to sit and chat with a woman and not have a trail of paparazzi stalk them or have to try to impress her with his money was, well, he'd given up on meeting that ridiculous standard months ago.

To simply enjoy talking to Ivy without her expecting a thing from him was refreshing.

She read the calendar square, "Read a book

in a genre you would normally avoid. So, what's that? Mystery? Science fiction? Self-help?"

"None of the above." He dug out the tattered paperback he'd purchased at the secondhand shop down the street and set it on the table.

Her gasp made him look around to ensure no one was watching them. Seriously, the cover was lurid peach and purple.

"Are you kidding me?" She picked up the book and fanned the pages. "Romance? And Loretta Chase? I love this story!"

The book title had called to him: *Lord of Scoundrels*. And while he'd been sheepish about selecting it, the clerk, an elder woman with bright violet hair—hex code B618CB—and half spectacles, had given him an enthusiastic recommendation.

"I read the first two chapters in the store, and I have to admit, it is good. I like how the author shows the hero as a kid in the beginning, so you know what it was like for him growing up."

He also related to that neglected, battered, and desperate child in the story. But that was a story Wolf kept close to his vest. No woman wanted to hear about his tough past. They preferred him in expensive suits, freely swiping his black credit card.

"You read two chapters in the store? How long were you there?"

"I'm a speed reader. It'll take me about an hour to finish the story. Figure I'll put away a few more chapters while I'm here."

"You really are switching things up. And a romance."

"Guys can read romance," he added defensively.

"Oh, I know they can. You just don't seem the type…" She shook her head. "Sorry. I wouldn't want anyone to presume anything about me, either. I am not what I appear on the surface."

He suspected as much about her. But how to really delve beneath her exterior? Because he wanted to learn more about Ivy, but without having to emotionally commit or fend off a court case. Was that asking too much? Probably. He'd never had a friendship with a woman, so navigating what was going on between them was a challenge beyond anything listed on a little calendar square.

"I'm happy you're enjoying the story," she offered. "You will fall in love with the couple, I promise."

"Thanks. And thanks again for talking to me like…"

"Like?"

"Like a normal person. I just…" Feeling his muscles tense, he wanted to close off the sudden need to express his desire for connection to her. So he did. "It's weird for me. New York is a weird city. It's so confined. And I'm either at work or at some celebrity function running away from the paparazzi."

"Estelle mentioned something about the paparazzi. She's the owner," Ivy explained. "She said there used to be days the customers could barely make it past the wall of photographers eager to get a shot of you. She's so relieved your love life has—er. Sorry."

Wolf shook his head. Even the coffee shop owner knew about his horrendous luck with women?

"I shouldn't have said that," she added. "Your private life is your business. I'm just sorry you have to endure things like crazy photographers trying to get a photo of you."

"I'm glad they've gone away. For now. But as soon as I start dating?" He shook his head. "They'll be back."

"Well, I hope it doesn't make you swear off dating forever. We humans are, by nature, in need of connection."

Connection was something he craved despite his finding it difficult to form such connections. It was the way he'd been raised. He'd learned to survive on his own, and welcoming others into his life wasn't so much a challenge as a lesson in protecting his boundaries. Feeling nothing was much easier than being vulnerable. As for romance? Caution was the key word after what he'd been through.

Ivy was suddenly summoned by Estelle's call across the café. "It's your brother."

"I have to take this. He's...not doing well lately. See you tomorrow?"

"For sure."

Her brother wasn't doing well? What was that about? And the fact that he was genuinely concerned surprised him. In a good way. He'd connected with Ivy. And that put a smile on his face for the rest of the day.

Dread curdled in Ivy's gut as she took the phone call in the back room.

"Ivan, what's up? Are you okay?"

"I don't want to scare you, Ivy, but the physical therapist wasn't able to make it in today and... I took a walk out to the park. But now... it's my eye. It's... I can't see out of it at all."

Her brother had been diagnosed with MS two months ago. His gait was unsteady and he'd begun to use a cane to get around. His doctor warned there were a litany of symptoms that may yet rise. The world had changed for him. And not in a good way.

"I'll be right there," she said.

"But you don't get off for another hour and a

half. I'm sorry. I should have waited until you got home, but… I'm still in the park… I know I can make it back…"

"Ivan, it's a fifteen-minute walk home. Hang on!"

She turned to find Estelle behind her, nodding. "Go ahead, sweetie. If it's your brother, he comes first. I've got two girls coming on shift soon."

"Thanks, Estelle. I'll put in extra time tomorrow."

"I know you will." Her boss hugged her. "Take that almost-expired cherry cake home with you as a treat for your brother."

"I will. See you tomorrow."

Should he or shouldn't he? Wolf's thoughts wandered as he typed. His mind was capable of focusing on a programming task while he simultaneously processed unrelated thoughts through his cortex. And he couldn't seem to keep Ivy out of his brain.

Not a terrible distraction.

Whether or not to ask her out was the question. He'd instituted his dating sabbatical because his lawyer had suggested he didn't need any more lawsuits or the bad publicity that came along with them. Yet he'd also given Wolf the name of a private investigator should he wish to date. He'd used him once, right before the sabbatical, and that woman had not checked out.

Clicking on the Concierge app in the upper right corner of his screen, Wolf searched for the PI's info and texted him a name, business name. That was the only information he had on Ivy. Then he hit *send*.

He sighed heavily, feeling some regret. It was what he had to do to avoid a lawsuit.

"I'm so sorry, Estelle. You stay home and take care of that flu. It's not fun being sick in the summertime."

Estelle sighed over the phone. She'd just let Ivy know she wouldn't be in today. They had four employees scheduled for the day so she wouldn't be missed. But First… would be fine without her.

"I'll work an hour later to cover until Valerie comes in," Ivy said.

"Thanks, sweetie. Is your brother doing okay?"

"He's got an appointment tomorrow with an ophthalmologist. He panicked yesterday, but it is something we need to address."

"I'm praying for him. Uh, there's one other thing. It's killing me, but my boyfriend is thrilled."

Ivy could not imagine what her boss would next say, so she listened.

"We were supposed to see the New York Philharmonic tonight. Mandalbrot is the featured violinist. Tony hates classical music, but you know I like to try new things. Anyway, do you want the tickets?"

"Oh? Uh…" Did she? Ivy had never been a fan of classical, yet she also didn't hate it. And wouldn't a night out be a nice vacation from her life? "I think I'd love to take them off your hands. Not sure who I can bring along with me, though."

"What about Ivan? You did say he gets around well enough with the cane. Might take his mind off the eye issue?"

Ivy chuckled. "Yes, he can get around, but I'm pretty sure hell can't get cold enough before Ivan would step inside an orchestral hall. He's heavy metal and alternative, all the way. I'll find someone. Maybe Valerie will want to go."

"Great. The concert starts at eight. It's at the Lincoln Center. It's not super fancy, but if you have a dress, wear that. I'll have a courier bring the tickets to the café right away. Call me if there are any problems."

"We'll be fine without you, Estelle. And checking the schedule, you have the weekend off, so that means you're all about snuggling up on the couch and watching *Practical Magic* for the next few days."

"Sounds kind of dreamy. Except the part

where I can't look at food without getting sick.
Too much information, sorry. Thanks, Ivy!"

Ivy hung up and Becky's shout alerted her the
front counter had a line waiting, so she hurried
out to meet the early-morning rush.

Just as Ivy was getting ready to punch out on
break, Wolf walked through the door and looked
for a table. Twelve-thirty? Really? She'd almost
thought she wouldn't see him today. That thought
had put her in a grumpy mood and caused her
to nearly spill a mango coconut smoothie on a
customer's lap.

The lunch rush had settled but still there were
no available tables, which left Wolf standing in
line, looking perplexed. When he reached the
counter, Ivy pushed in front of Valerie and told
him she'd pack his chocolate chip cake to go.

"Thanks. I guess I should stick to the earlier
hours. It's crowded in here."

"That's how the lunch rush goes! I have a
break now, so I'll bring it out to you. I'll meet
you outside?"

He gave her a grateful nod. "Sounds good."

She punched out, hung her apron, then grabbed
Wolf's order and met him out front.

"You want to walk?" he asked. "I'll share my
cake with you."

"Definitely—wait!" She remembered the call

from Estelle. "I think I'd better stick around the shop front. My boss sent a courier, and I need to receive it when it arrives."

"How about across the street?"

They settled on the bench under a maple tree with wide leaves that frothed halfway across the street. Ivy gleefully accepted the bigger half from Wolf when he divided the cake. She hadn't eaten since an early breakfast of burnt toast smeared with peanut butter with blueberries.

With crumbs licked from her fingers, and a sip of Wolf's coffee to wash it down, she then asked, "What's today's challenge?"

"Say yes to everything."

"Oh? That covers a lot. What have you said yes to so far?"

He cleared his throat and recited, marking off on his fingers as he did, "Next week off for Carol because her parents are in town visiting."

"Kind of you."

"We'll manage for a few days without her tendency to sing show tunes at the top of her lungs. Then I said yes to a round of boxing with the brute who occasionally comes into the gym."

"Oh, yeah? Who won?"

"Let's just say my bruises are covered by my clothes. But I did give him a good fight."

"Wow. I'm so impressed. Handsome and a skilled fighter. Uh… I mean…"

"I think you just called me handsome." His smile was liquid seduction. A blush warmed her ears. "I'll take it. And I just said yes to a pretty woman who asked me to meet her outside for a snack. That was a nice surprise."

Likewise. "Unexpected surprises are always fun."

"Really? You like surprises? I like knowing what's coming. To be prepared."

"No spontaneity for you?"

"Probably not." He offered her the last corner of his cake and she took it. "How long is your break?"

"I'm going to hang here to wait for the courier. Oh."

She was all about helping him with his calendar challenges. Dare she? It would be sneaky, since he had committed to the yes.

"Oh?" he prompted.

"I was just thinking about if I should dare go for another yes from you. Even despite your fear of spontaneity."

He turned to completely face her, resting an elbow on the back of the bench. Bemusement was an interesting emotion on him. But also charming. His virile intensity made her want to run her fingers through his thick beard—and tug him in for a kiss.

"Are you taking advantage of my inability to say no today?"

Was she? Maybe a little? It wasn't as if they were anything more than friends. It would mean nothing to him, and she needn't think of it as a date because she did not want to become tabloid fodder. Yet, Valerie was busy tonight, so...

All right, she dared!

"Estelle is sick and so gave me two tickets to a concert tonight. It's an orchestral performance at the Lincoln Center. I wonder if... Would you like to go with me?" And then she quickly added, "Just as friends, of course. Because I know you have the dating sabbatical going on."

He nodded quickly. "Friends. Of course, that's...us."

Was that reluctance for the invitation or something deeper in his pause? Ivy did not regret the ask, but she would be disappointed if she earned his first no of the day.

"You don't have to say yes if the idea of listening to violins and cellos sounds super boring."

"Actually, I do have to say yes. But also, it's not killing me to say it. I listen to all kinds of music. What time is it?"

"At eight. I can meet you out front of the Lincoln Center around seven-thirty?"

"I can pick you up."

"No, I don't want to ask too much of you. And besides, well…"

Besides what? His picking her up would definitely feel like a date. Going Dutch was the only way she could do it and make it work for her strangely pining heart.

"It's how I want to do it."

"Sounds workable. Tonight! What should I wear? Is this a fancy shindig?"

"Not super fancy, but maybe a suit?"

"I can do that." He tossed his cup and it landed in the nearby trash bin.

At that moment the bike courier parked before But First…

"I think that's the tickets." Ivy stood and rushed across the street, calling back, "See you later!"

CHAPTER FOUR

HAVING LIVED IN New York City four years, Wolf had gotten invited to many events at famous buildings and venues, but he'd never been inside the Lincoln Center. The outer façade, a travertine and glass box, was brilliantly lit at night, inviting all who passed to gaze at the building that looked like a fallen star among the surrounding stuffy brick and limestone buildings. Inside, the David Geffen Hall had been recently gutted and remodeled, and he loved the warm, natural wood interior. Their balcony seats directly overlooked the orchestra. It felt cozy and not too pretentious. He could relax here. And he needed to do that. Because this was a new experience for him.

That experience being attending a concert that played music he'd rarely listened to, but more importantly, attending it with a woman who was not a girlfriend. He wasn't sure how to parse it all. Because Ivy felt like someone with whom he wanted to be more than a friend.

Should he stop looking at her, inhaling her, wondering how soft her skin might be should they kiss? Of course. Because his instincts warned: *Beware. Don't let her in. Remain cautious.*

And yet... Just how gorgeous could a woman, who seemed to be wearing barely a hint of makeup save some mascara, be? She wore a sleek white knee-length dress that revealed shoulders and a diamond of her bare back. Her hair was up in a tight, smooth ponytail. *De rigueur* for her. Higher on her head than she usually wore it at But First... It looked classy. But also controlled. Like she wasn't comfortable with letting down her hair. He could imagine her full, lush hair spilling to mid-back. Tickling her bare skin. And she smelled like those treats he should have cut out of his diet for the calendar challenge.

He leaned in, taking a moment to inhale and linger in her aura. Her scent was so soft, forcing him to be still and crowd out all other sensations. *There.* Like a warm summer day near a garden. But as well, sultry, teasing of moans of satisfying sex.

Don't do it, man. Keep your distance.

Right. Because letting a woman into his life never ended well.

He muttered, "I've never done this before."

"What's that?" She leaned closer, their heads nearly touching.

She smells like a garden, not the promise of sex. And don't forget it!

"Listened to a live orchestra performance."

"They'll be performing Beethoven's *Fifth* tonight. You'll recognize that one."

"Will I?"

She slid a hand over his and patted it. Such an easy, natural move. Her skin was soft and warm. "You will. Trust me, this could be fun."

"I'm game for anything."

She turned to study his face. Eyes like blue icebergs were cool yet so full of life. He could stare into her eyes all day and forget all about the bits and bytes that made up his world.

"You know the color of your eyes is 74D4E7?" he blurted out.

"I—what?"

"It's a hex code for programming colors." He repeated the code.

"I didn't know my eyes could be labeled with a code. Kind of cool," she whispered as the lights suddenly dimmed. "I know tonight is just a means to help you with your challenge, but I haven't had a night out in so long. I appreciate you doing me this favor."

"No problem." A favor sounded safer than a date. Yet, why did his self-imposed boundaries suddenly feel so confining?

As the musicians took their seats on the stage

and the house lights went down, Wolf's brain chastised him for missing an opportunity. Could this have been a real date? He shouldn't have to close off his life from others just because the press hounded him.

Thing was, all he wanted was for someone to see him. To value him. And that had never happened. Ever.

Crossing his arms, Wolf nodded. Just a challenge, this night. It could never be anything more.

After the concert, they took an Uber to a restaurant a few blocks away from Ivy's brownstone. They ordered dessert and shared a lush chocolate caramel bomb cake. Ivy was aware of her white dress with every bite she quickly maneuvered to her mouth. No spills. Points for her! Wolf got some caramel in his beard but before she could reach for it, he swiped it with a napkin. No points for him. Just as well. She felt off-balance, unsure how to act toward him. He was a friend, sure, but—did she want this to become more?

Of course you do. And stop using the excuse that you're observing him as if he's an insect under the microscope. You're attracted to him. You want to know if he can tick off all the items on your perfect man list.

Guilty as charged.

The restaurant was crowded, and it was difficult to hear each other so when they finished eating they immediately left. With her place so close, they strolled down the sidewalk, shoulder to shoulder. The night was warm and the air humid with scents of tarmac and newly unfurled spring leaves. Walking alongside Wolf felt like where she wanted to be.

His outer actions lent to some kind of dateness going on. Did friends walk down the street nudging each other's shoulders? Catching each other's gaze across a bite of cake? Telling her what code her eyes were? He confused her. And she didn't like to be strung along if his only goal was to use her to better his life via some daily challenge.

But who was she fooling? He'd been clear about not wanting to date. And why did she need this night to be more than friends? She was reaching for stars. Trying to fit Wolf into the parameters of that silly list she'd made with Estelle was just a fairy tale. And fairy tales were for children and hopeless romantics. Of which, she was not.

If she wanted to date and have a sex life, she could attract a willing man. She didn't have the time for it right now. Or the emotional heart space. All attention had to be focused on her brother.

And yet at the moment, all attention veered

toward the overwhelming presence walking alongside her. He filled the air and she felt protected, as if he wrapped himself around her and occupied the air she breathed. It felt immense. Promising.

Just friends, she reminded herself inwardly.

They arrived in front of the brownstone Ivan was house-sitting. Across the street, a small park with a dog area and a few benches beckoned. Ivy veered toward the green lawn, and they sat on a bench. Not far from them a streetlight glowed. Somewhere crickets chirped. It was almost midnight, and there were no walkers. They had the park to themselves.

"That's your brother's place?" Wolf asked.

"Yes. It's really nice inside. Very modern and minimalist. He has it until the beginning of January."

"Has it? It's…not his?"

"Oh, no. That place would cost a fortune to rent. Ivan, well, he's created his own profession. He's always been a nomad, a guy who likes to adventure and see new places. He figured out a way to do it as inexpensively as possible. Also, he likes to push his boundaries, challenge himself to live on as little as possible, make a small dent in the environment."

"Noble. But what's the profession he created?"

"He's an international house sitter. He'll watch

someone's house for a week or even months when they go on vacation. In this case, it's nearly a year. I understand the owners are traveling the world via sailboat. So Ivan gets free rent, a place to stay, and usually only has to pay utilities. And he's a master at finding short-term work in the area to cover those expenses. He even does volunteer work. He's been house-sitting probably five years."

"That's resourceful. What's his current job?"

"Well." Ivy dropped her shoulders.

"Does he have one? Or is he doing volunteer work?"

"It's complicated."

He leaned against the back of the bench, bringing up an ankle to rest across his opposite knee. "I recall you saying something about caring for your brother? Is it okay to ask about that?"

Ivy inhaled, fortifying herself for the information that she rarely told anyone. Estelle knew her situation. The interesting friendship that had formed between her and Wolf felt trustworthy. At the very least, he was expressing interest, and that made her feel safe. So why not tell him?

"I was intending to move to Switzerland two months ago."

"For a job?"

"Yes, I got accepted by the Mercer Institute to join their research team on Insect Systematics."

"Okay, wait." He turned to face her. With the streetlight beaming across his face, Ivy memorized the exact shade of his eyes. "I thought I attended a concert with a barista tonight. But you're talking about bugs and research. So that's not just your weird T-shirt obsession? Who *are* you?"

Ivy chuckled. In a moment of villainous teasing she said, "Wouldn't you like to know."

He caught the levity and countered with a, "It'll go a lot easier for you if you spill the beans now."

A waggle of his brow reminded her how easily she could succumb to any suggestion he might make regarding intimacy between them.

Just friends, remember. He said yes to you tonight because he had to. That's all there is to this. Stick to field observations.

"It's nothing so interesting as a supervillain," she said. "I'm an entomologist. I studied environmental biologics. I'd love to secure a position studying the population biology of, well, any endangered species. I adore a fuzzy bee or dragonfly, and don't get me started on the order *coleoptera*. That's beetles."

He smoothed a hand along his jaw, mirth evident in his eyes. But he didn't say anything, so she rambled on some more. Because right now her nerves translated to talking.

"After I finished college, I got a job working

for the Maine forestry service. Eighty percent of the work was outdoors, which I love. I traveled around the state tracking invasive species, tagging moths, and talking at events for kids, but I've always wanted to venture to new places. Across the ocean, to rain forests, deserts, wherever bugs can be found. I'd had the Mercer Institute on my list since walking into college. After three long but successful Zoom interviews, I was offered the job. It was a dream come true."

"A dream that you're…not living right now?"

Another sigh rippled down her spine, settling uneasily in her gut. "My brother, Ivan, has been feeling odd for years. Low energy, sleeping more than his usual five or six hours a night, muscles kinking up on him. Some days he couldn't even get out of bed. And that was strange because he's an athlete. He had plans to ride his cycle across the United States until—well."

Ivy realized her story was complicated. She had never told anyone the full version. It was all still so fresh and happening to her day by day. Yet with two glasses of wine swirling in her brain, she decided to go for it.

"Okay, here's the full history of Ivy Quinn. Shortened because I don't want the audience to fall asleep."

"I would never fall asleep listening to you,"

he said quickly. "Read to me from one of your dry college textbooks? I'm there."

"I'll remember that. Anyway, my parents died in a boating accident when I was twelve. Ivan was eighteen. He was one month away from beginning that bike ride. He intended to zig-zag across the US, hitting every state, and then take Canada back to Maine, where we grew up. But after we lost our parents, that plan had to be shelved. Ivan stepped up to become the head of the household. He took care of me. Got a real job so he could pay the bills. We inherited the house and land. Selling some of the land kept us going until I graduated. I thought then that Ivan would go on that ride, but instead he suggested we sell the house and use the money to really start our lives. And pay for my college. Ivan put most of his share in savings and started doing his house-sitting thing, and I finished college. Flash forward years later and I got the job offer. And Ivan was finally diagnosed with MS."

Wolf blew out a breath. "I'm sorry. That's rough. I know a guy who has that. He…well, he's in a wheelchair."

"Some can have mild cases and function quite well. Others are not so lucky. I'm learning there are so many versions and varying stages of the diagnosis. Ivan is at an early stage where doc-tors believe he may be able to function quite well with it, but he could also take an extreme left turn and—" She bowed her head.

Wolf clasped her hand. The heat of his touch startled her. A gentle squeeze made her swallow back a tear. She wasn't a tearful woman. And she would not be so in front of this man.

"Ivan is currently moving about with the help of a cane. His vision in one eye has blurred recently. I moved from Maine to stay with him. It was the least I could do after all he had sacrificed for me after our parents' deaths. I feel like I owe him that much. I want to make sure he gets good health insurance, finds the right doctors, doesn't have to—do it all on his own. So we're taking it one day at a time now."

"You're a very good little sister. Sounds like you two take care of your own. I'm proud of you."

That statement loosened a tear in her eye, and before she could stop it, it spilled. Ivy caught it with her fingertip. "Thank you."

It had been a long time since anyone had affirmed anything she had done. No parents to congratulate her at high school or college graduation. It felt good to hear it from Wolf. But in a bittersweet way.

"Sorry," she said. "I never cry. This is silly."

"Don't be ashamed. You're one strong woman,

Ivy. I'm glad you trusted me to tell me that. It means a lot. And I don't say that lightly."

"Enough of the sob story. I'm doing just fine. Ivan is the one who needs the support right now. We were able to hire a physical therapist to help him navigate the progression of his condition. She stops by a few times a week. But since Ivan doesn't have a real job, he doesn't have health insurance. We need to plan for that future when the last of our parents' house sale money is gone. I just want him to get the help he requires to live and function, you know? I have work that's, well, it doesn't pay as much as the Mercer Institute, but it puts food on the table and pays for some of his medications. As well, it gets me out in the community. I need the interaction. I like talking to people."

"But you'd be much happier studying bugs."

"Much." Now she laughed softly. "So I'm the crazy bug lady. I know I'll get back to doing what I love someday. But for now, I'm content to help my brother any way I can. I just hope we can get his life on a track that works for him before he has to give up this fabulous brownstone. And if he can eventually return to traveling, that would be amazing. I'm not sure how that's possible, though."

"Maybe if he had a traveling partner? A health professional accompanying him?"

"Sounds perfect, but also expensive. We'll see. I try not to worry too much about things. I like to stay positive for Ivan's sake."

"Your positivity is catchy. There's a reason I've stopped in at But First… every morning since you started working there. I wasn't much of a coffee man before that."

She turned to study his face now. "Really?"

He shrugged. "What can I say? I guess I can't keep away from you. And look at us? We've become friends."

Friends. Coming out of his mouth, it sounded like a dirty word to her. When everything about Wolf made her senses stand up and take notice. It would be so easy to lean against him, tilt her head onto his shoulder, and just…see what might happen next. He was a sexy man, handsome and smart and…he checked off a lot of the items on that list she'd made. Surely, he believed in love.

Oh, why did her heart have to struggle so with her common sense?

Best to avoid asking him about his belief in love. It wasn't an appropriate question for their friendly evening.

"What about you?" she asked. "What strange or horrible history are you keeping close to the vest?"

"You don't want to know."

"I think you owe me."

"Maybe?" He did that straight shoulders thing that clued her in to something inside him shutting down or changing. Becoming less open. "Let's focus on your stuff tonight. Caring for your brother is a lot to handle. And if you ever need a hand to hold or an ear to listen, I'm there."

"That means a lot. Thank you. It is late. I should probably get inside and check on Ivan. Thanks for coming along with me tonight. For saying yes."

"Honestly? Forget about the stupid calendar. I'd go anywhere with you, Ivy."

"I'll keep that in mind next time I want to escape my life for an evening."

He grasped her hand and kissed the back of it. A surprising move that stuttered her breaths. "Please do. Let me walk you to the door."

At the top of the brick stair before the brownstone door, Ivy paused and turned to him. She stuck her hand out to shake, thinking how much she'd rather lift her head and close her eyes. Wait for a kiss. To know the touch of his mouth on hers. Their breaths mingling. Bodies melding…

The sudden firm squeeze of her hand brought her back to reality with the sad exhale of a deflating balloon.

"Goodnight, Ivy," he said. "See you tomorrow."

"Of course."

He took the steps swiftly, and as he walked

along the sidewalk, he turned once to wave. She waved back. A heavy sigh deflated her shoulders.

"What are you doing wrong?" she muttered.

Of course, she knew it hadn't been a date. "Just friends" had to become her motto.

But really? Was she that unattractive to the man that he hadn't at least tried to make a move on her? Should she have been more forthright, perhaps initiating more intimate contact? It hadn't felt right at the crowded concert. And in the park the conversation about Ivan's condition hadn't been the perfect moment either.

Dare she imagine she could move beyond friends and break down Wolf's walls to capture the rogue billionaire's attention? And if she did, did she want it? Could she manage a love affair while also caring for her brother? She did not want to bring media snoops into Ivan's life merely because she had been seen with Wolf. He didn't need that stress on top of all the medical stress he was dealing with.

Besides, it seemed Wolf's relationships were accompanied by paparazzi and a fast ending.

Contrary, Ivy was all about true love and happy endings.

CHAPTER FIVE

ON SUNDAY MORNINGS, his first stop was the gym. Wolf had lifted for half an hour then did some boxing with the heavy bag. Now, following a shower, he stood in the elevator alone, riding it to the top floor. He enjoyed being in the office on weekends. The quiet allowed him to focus.

What did give his head a dizzy swirl was thoughts of Ivy in that stark white dress. All eyes had been on her as they'd walked through the concert hall to their seats. He'd dated some beautiful women. Some of them very smart. A model here and there. The choices in New York were endless. And it wasn't so much that he had to put himself out there as they seemed to be attracted to him like flies to flypaper.

He was over being sticky.

And yet.

How long *did* he intend this sabbatical from dating to continue? He'd never drawn an end date. Yes, dating was dangerous. He suspected it was so because women tended to be blinded by his dollar signs, never truly connecting to the man he was on an emotional level. Most of them, anyway. And if he were honest with himself? That little boy inside him who never got any attention growing up loved getting it from the women he dated. Yet, it never felt true, or genuine.

Should he jump back in, there was always the chance of getting burned, no matter what rules he made regarding dating, or how long he tried to avoid relationships. He'd sighted a couple paparazzi outside the hall last night. He didn't want to do the chase anymore. And he certainly didn't want to put any woman through that craziness.

And yet, Ivy was different. Spending time with her did not feel surface or material as had his previous relationships. He'd never gone slow with a woman.

His heart craved emotional regard, the knowing comfort of a real connection.

He'd text Ivy later, see what she was up to. Thank her again for helping him out with his "yes" day. And if the moment took him, maybe he'd ask her out for real.

Because he was shaking things up, wasn't he? Trying new challenges? Trusting new experiences? Ivy didn't seem the least interested in his money. She had been the one to ask him to the concert. A bold move, if he considered it.

Or was that simply her plot to snag him? Get him interested. Then, wham! What can you do for me, Zeigler? You've got money. Show me how much you want to keep me in your life.

Wolf hated to think in those terms. But he'd lived those terms. So he'd be cautious where things went with Ivy. Yet, he had to start trusting his judgment sooner or later.

He strolled into his office and tossed his workout duffel onto the floor then picked up the calendar to read the day's challenge.

"Seriously?"

He rubbed a hand over the back of his head. Well, that certainly would be a challenge. Guess he wouldn't be seeing Ivy after all.

Instead, he took out his phone and snapped a photo of the calendar page.

Ivy wandered into the kitchen in her two-piece silky pajamas. A rim of marabou sewn around the ankle hems had worn away long ago. So she liked to do the glamour thing once in a while. Despite her love for bugs, she was a girly girl at heart.

Ivan was still asleep, so she'd start breakfast. Using the shiny copper cookware that hung from a rack over the center island was fun. The sleek, modern kitchen made her feel as though she were on a cooking show, creating savory dishes for so many watching.

After breakfast she'd use her day off to continue the search for affordable insurance. For a man who thrived on physical activity and never slowing down, this diagnosis had been particularly hard on Ivan. Even with his symptoms aside, he wasn't designed to sit still. And while the physical therapist did accompany him on walks in the park across the street, that may not last forever. Ivy hoped it did. Perhaps even that the exercise would help him to improve. She'd done a little reading on the disease and some websites where fellow MS patients chatted and posted diets and exercise routines that actually improved their symptoms.

Wolf's mention of finding a traveling professional health assistant intrigued her. Did something like that exist? If Ivan was able to travel, that could prove to be his best bet to have as close to normal a life as possible. She added that to her list of things to check out.

There were studies he might qualify for that would offer him free medical treatment—experimental, of course. She had created a list over the weeks she'd been here and would start filling out applications for Ivan's acceptance. It was a move in the right direction.

But as she cracked some eggs over the frying pan, her thoughts segued from Ivan's dire future to last night. It had felt good to get dressed up and sit beside Wolf. The music and the company had energized her. Touched the woman inside her that loved being seen by a man. And it had made her forget about Ivan and his troubles, if only for an evening.

And while guilt prodded at her, a part of her did a little happy dance because she'd allowed herself to enjoy last night. Until Wolf had asked about Ivan. Really, when did she cry? In that quiet moment on the park bench, it had felt as if she'd unloaded a heavy weight. She'd needed to tell someone. And that he'd held her hand meant the world to her.

Now, would he call? He had no reason to. Last night had been a transaction. Alas, they were just friends. Just another man in the wild she must observe and learn about.

"No emotional energy for a relationship, remember?" she quietly reminded.

Her phone pinged with a text message. Ivy scrambled the eggs with a spatula while checking the screen. Wolf had sent a photo of… She laughed when she read the calendar page for today. *Spend the day alone. Go within. Listen to what's inside.*

And he had added:

Great to spend time with you last night. See you
Monday morning?

She texted back:

For sure.

Spending the day alone seemed like something Wolf might find easy to do. But she also
knew he did like to be out in the world, not
necessarily face-to-face with others, but beside
them, especially when it related to business. No
wonder it had bothered him so much what the
office thought about his past romances. He put
a lot of weight in what others thought of him.

Whereas Ivy cared little if a person liked her.
So long as they were not hateful or falsely ac-
commodating. Perhaps Wolf's past relationships had pushed him too far into the noise and
busyness of social media, entertainment, status,
and…well, he'd mentioned the money.

What she could do with the money Wolf had
would be phenomenal. First, she'd get Ivan the
best medical care. Then, she'd move to Switzerland and take the job. Though, she knew that job
was no longer available. Then? She'd buy herself
a small but cozy place to live. Or maybe she'd
get a backpack and travel the world, seeking insects in the rainforest and accepting jobs where

she could find them, following in her brother's nomadic footsteps. Yes, money would change her life. But it wouldn't necessarily make it easy.

She wondered what Wolf did with all his money. News media and tabloids liked to write about the rich and famous. But when she had the idea to look into him a little more, she shook her head. She liked the Wolf she knew right now. And whatever she learned about him would be what he wanted her to know.

Though she was curious about his eye color. After sliding the eggs onto a plate, she searched online for hex codes.

On Monday, Wolf's calendar challenged him to expose a mistake to a friend. So while on a walk along the pier with Ivy during his lunch hour, he bought her a corndog and they shared a large cherry frosty that she insisted she could never finish, but she did make a concerted effort at consuming her share.

"A mistake?" she asked when he told her about the challenge. "It should be not too devastating, but not too simple. Something middle ground."

He leaned back on the bench, his shoulder hugging hers. Before them the Hudson's bean soup waters wavered and crashed against the docks. Beyond the pungent scent he picked up coffee beans. Did she notice that he took a few seconds to inhale her with an unobtrusive tilt of his head to the side? If she did, she didn't say anything.

"I've made plenty of mistakes," he said. Like swearing off dating. Because really? Gorgeous woman sitting so close he wanted to kiss her. "But one I do regret was when I was fifteen. Me and a couple guys from the foster home snuck out to the shed and gave one another tattoos. With a hot needle, not a tattoo gun."

"That sounds like something a teenage boy would do. Where is it? Show it to me?"

He propped an ankle over his knee and lifted his pant leg to expose it. In blurred blue ink a makeshift hand with the middle finger lifted.

Ivy touched his ankle as she inspected. Wolf sucked in a breath. Her skin against his was the conduit to something so intense. Every time she touched him he felt an erotic thrill.

"That's hilarious," she said.

"More like stupid. I haven't had the desire to get inked since."

"I don't know, I could see you with a wild animal or tribal something or other. Or how about your namesake?" She shrugged when he shook his head. "I have a couple tattoos."

"Do you?"

"One is on the back of my shoulder." She

scooted forward on the bench and tugged down the sleeve of her T-shirt. "Can you see?"

He spread his hand across her back and tugged the shirt down to expose a beautifully rendered metallic green and shimmery copper tattoo of what looked like… "A beetle?"

"*Chrysochroa aurora*," she said. "It's one of my favorites. I also have a *calopterygidea*, which is a jewelwing damselfly, on my hip. I think it would be awesome to be covered with fluttering insects."

"You really do love your bugs. What inspired you to entomology?"

"I've chased and studied them since I was a kid. They are nature's works of art. Also, my dad was a wildlife biologist. You know we have only classified and discovered less than thirty percent of the entire insect species? I want to travel to the rainforest someday to hunt for butterflies. Finding the blushing phantom butterfly is my dream. It has the most incredible rose-red coloring on its mostly transparent wings." She tilted her head down and smiled up at him through her lashes. "I have big dreams."

"About little things," he added. "I hope you get to do all of that, Ivy. And send me the pictures when you do."

"I will. I'm also polishing my photography skills. Have you seen close-up macro shots of bugs? They are amazing. They capture all the microscopic details like the *ommatidium* and detailed mouthparts. A fine jungle of hairs on a carapace. I could stare at them for hours. But I'd never catch and kill an insect just to take its picture."

"Don't entomologists kill bugs for research?"

She winced. "We try not to. Sometimes it is necessary. Especially in a big netting situation."

At that pronouncement her eyes took him in. As if wondering how large a net she might need for him? The thought made him smile.

"You'll get your chance to do everything you dream about." He clasped her hand. "Your brother will get the help he needs and become self-sufficient, then you'll be off to the wilds of Brazil to photograph butterflies."

"Ivan is so positive it sometimes freaks me out. There are days I find this all so overwhelming. And he just sits there with a smile. I know this is devastating for him, but he'll never say that to me."

"He sounds like a strong person. Like you. If you need anything, you must let me know."

"Thank you. You said something about you and some guys from a foster home. Did you… live in a foster home?"

Wolf slouched against the bench and stretched out his legs. No woman had ever seemed to care enough about him to ask about his history. He would never completely trust any woman, but Ivy came close to opening his heart for a careful peek into his past. And he wanted to tell her. He needed to share that part of himself with someone. Perhaps as a feeler to see if she really could be trusted. Dare he?

"You don't have to tell me," she said. "I understand you are guarded. You must have to be with the world wanting to photograph your every move."

She understood that part of his life. Bless her.

"I lived in foster care since birth." He glanced to see her expression. A calm, interested pair of 74D4E7s. He'd never felt more seen than when Ivy was with him.

"My parents, I was told, were killed in a plane crash. My mother was nine months pregnant. After she had been pulled from the crash, they performed an emergency caesarean and rescued me."

She took his hand and held it without saying anything. In that moment something tugged at the back of Wolf's throat and the corners of his eyes. Crybabies got bullied and beat up. The smart kid worked hard to earn a few bucks' allowance and then paid the bullies to stay away from him.

"I lived in a total of nine foster homes," he said. "Once a kid gets older, their chances of adoption go way down. I was always a kid who lived inside his head too, so I hadn't the talent to put on a show when a potential permanent family came to visit. I left the CPS system when I was seventeen. Found a couch to sleep on at a friend's house. Spent my days with my nose to the screen. Still doing that." He laughed.

"How did you develop an interest in coding?"

Ah, now there was a topic he enjoyed talking about. And that she'd not lingered on the worst part of his history? Another point for Ivy Quinn.

"I used to help my foster moms with their passwords and computer problems. That would earn me some time on the computer. I discovered the hacker boards and the private net. I instantly understood. I caught a math teacher coding one afternoon while he was on a lunch break. He allowed me to look over his shoulder and I pointed out a mistake he had made. From there he allowed me to spend time programming after school. Taught me a lot. He was the only person who ever made me feel as though I could accomplish something."

Wolf laughed nervously. "I mean, well, I don't want it to sound like my life was so terrible..." Even though it hadn't been all that great.

"I love that a teacher took you under his wing," she said. "That's so important. Teachers can shape the trajectory of a child's life. So you really are a coding savant?"

"Yes, it's served me well. I created my own tech empire. But in the process, I learned not to trust people. Well, I guess you could say I've always been that way. Never had an opportunity to learn what trust really meant."

"Because of the way you grew up, you have boundaries. I respect that."

Wolf felt that comment deep in his chest. A validation of sorts. And issued without pretense or an ulterior desire to get on his good side.

"What gave you the idea for Concierge?"

"Just trying to keep my life together, the few bits I could carry from couch to couch. I wanted a means to always know what I had and where it was. I guess that was the kid in me that was used to guarding the few things he owned. I actually coded a few apps by the time I was seventeen when I was still couch surfing. I got my first apartment when I was eighteen and had an offer for my first app on the table. That app was Zang."

"I remember that one. It didn't seem to last very long, though."

"It wasn't designed to. It was a data collection app. Data is king. Companies pay big bucks to know everything about the consumer, even things you probably don't know yourself."

"Really? Like what things does a company know about me that I don't know?"

"Your interests. Your dreams. Your goals."

"That's unbelievable."

"It is, but not unattainable if you have some ones and zeros programmed to access how long you pause when you're scrolling through social media apps and how you respond to those silly quizzes and rampant advertising."

"Oh, my God, I'm never filling out one of those quizzes again."

"Good call. Protect your data." He shook his head and chuckled. "Sorry. I could talk tech all day. So, I told you one of my mistakes. An ugly one, for sure. Will you tell me one of yours?"

"A mistake? Hmm..."

Everyone made mistakes, but Wolf found it hard to believe this perfect woman could make any serious transgression beyond a screwed-up latte recipe.

A burst of wind off the Hudson warmed his face and tickled his ear, until he realized it was Ivy's hair brushing his skin. He closed his eyes, savoring the sensation.

Just kiss her already!

Dare he? It felt...not right. The moment needed to be bigger, yes? Maybe? Hell, he wanted to do things right with Ivy. Not have a replay of every relationship that had exploded in his face since moving to New York. She was not a woman to be rushed.

Finally, she said, "I'm not sure I made the right choice in refusing the offer to work at Mercer."

"But you wanted to be with your brother, to help him."

"I did, and I do. But my finances took a hit with that choice. Would it have been better had I gone to Switzerland and arranged for Ivan to receive the care long distance? I don't know. I feel as if it was a good decision, but then some days I think it was a mistake. I passed up a well-paying position."

"Is your brother in such a place that he needs twenty-four-seven care?"

"No. And actually, he's been on his own up until I arrived. But with his vision giving him trouble—well, I want to help him navigate this diagnosis. He's spent his life on his own, defying challenges. He really deserves some compassion and assistance right now."

"I get that. What if…someone were to offer to pay for your brother's medical care?"

"Oh, I don't think that will ever happen," she started and then she paused, looking quickly to him.

Wolf raised a brow and pointed at his chest.

She shook her head furiously and stood. "No, absolutely not."

"But—"

"I don't want to discuss it. Between the two of us, Ivan and I have enough for a year or so. And by then I'll have figured things out, perhaps gotten the perfect job."

"Sure, but until then…"

"Wolf, I…" She tugged out her phone and checked the screen. "I should get back to work." She turned and started walking quickly back toward the building.

Wolf managed to toss the drink cup in the garbage but the corndog wrapper missed, so he doubled back to pick it up and make the can, but that gave her a head start. "Ivy!"

He had opened up to her about growing up. Had bared his soul. And he'd felt as though she had listened without judgment. So how could she switch her emotions so quickly and storm off like that? Couldn't they have a simple conversation regarding his desire to help? The money meant nothing to him.

That thought made him stop, while Ivy crossed the street ahead of him. If the money meant so little, then why was he still here in New York, a city that seemed to press in on his very skeletal structure with immense force, squeezing out his privacy and self-confidence?

You're in a rut.

And he needed to do more than tearing pages

off a calendar. He needed to step up and take control of his life. Walk toward the life that would make him happy.

He let Ivy go. He'd talk to her later. Apologize for trying to help. Which seemed counterintuitive. But he understood. She was a proud woman. It would be difficult for her to accept charitable assistance.

Just as it was difficult for him to surrender his fears and open his heart again to a relationship?

CHAPTER SIX

IVY HAD PUNCHED out before her walk with Wolf. She didn't need to return to But First… But her anger had clouded her senses, so now she veered toward her brother's home and, before going inside, decided to sit on the front steps and cool down.

She rarely got angry. And if so, usually she hid it with a cool demeanor. But Wolf's offer to pay for Ivan's medical bills had hit her in the gut. It had felt solicitous. Though, now that she considered it, Wolf may not have meant it in such a manner. Had he been genuinely trying to help?

She did not need the man's money. She and Ivan were perfectly capable of handling his medical expenses on their own. They'd not taken the million dollars offered to them by the boat manufacturer after their parents' death because, after discussing it, both she and Ivan had felt it was hush money. Don't tell anyone there had been a delayed recall on that part that could have very well been the result of the accident. They'd walked away from that deal with their heads held high.

And Ivy wanted to feel the same now, having refused the offer from Wolf. But for some reason, she was torn. Sure, they had money remaining from the house sale, but that wouldn't last longer than a year or two. Yet, damn it, both she and Ivan were smart. They could handle this. Many people handled worse medical diagnoses. As soon as she could find Ivan the proper medical insurance, that would help immensely.

It had been a spur-of-the-moment offer from Wolf. He'd think about it and realize it had been offensive.

She checked her phone. No text from Wolf. Did she expect one? It wasn't as though they were a couple.

You want him to be more than a friend, and you know it!

Was it possible to juggle Ivan's care with her own self-care? Which suggested having a relationship with a man who excited and interested her. Beyond just friends. Of course, anything was possible. But she'd moved to New York specifically to help Ivan. Would it be fair to him to divide her time? For that matter, would it be fair to Wolf?

Not like she had any chance with the man anyway.

Leaning forward and catching her chin in hand, Ivy zoned out on the park greenery across the street. Just when she'd thought he'd begun to let down his emotional walls—telling her about growing up in the foster system—suddenly he'd closed up.

Rather, she had closed up. Why had she acted that way after he'd opened up to her? She didn't want to ruin what they had created between them. She couldn't imagine what it would be like to have never known a real family. At the very least, she had enjoyed twelve wonderful years with her parents. They had taught her much, and she had emulated her wildlife biologist father's work ethic aimed toward curiosity mixed with a fascination for nature. How many times had they gone on butterfly hunts with nets in hand and notebooks to sketch their finds? Her dad had always returned any caught insect back to the wild. The times they had found a dead bug nestled in fallen leaves they had taken it home, pinned it, and he had taught her how to look up information on the species online or in his small library.

As a kindergarten teacher, Ivy's mother had been the more studious of the pair. Teaching her how to cook, be practical with her buying decisions, and not to succumb to the teenage angst that demanded social submission. When most kids had been staring at their cell phones, Ivy and Ivan had been staring at nature or running through the woods. The rule had been no phone until you could pay the bill yourself. Ivy had proudly walked her own path through high school and had always felt her parents' angels on her shoulder as she did so.

"I miss you," she whispered to her parents. "I wish you were here to help Ivan through this now."

Had her brother wished for the same thing immediately following their deaths when he had no choice but to step up and become the parent figure in her life? Probably. Ivy had always been cognizant of his sacrifice for her. Which is why staying with him while he figured out this MS diagnosis had been a no-brainer for her.

She looked at her phone again. Wolf may have been perplexed at her sudden need to rush away from him. It had been a stupid move. She should have talked to him, calmly explained that she did not need his charity. End of it. Move on.

Opening the message app, she started to text him…

I'm sorry…

Ivy tapped delete. Texting was no way to apologize. It had to be in person. And not in the coffee shop, either. She wrote another text.

Could we meet later for something to eat?

Waiting, she saw the three dots pop up as he replied.

Meet me at the Korean barbecue down the street from you at seven?

Yes, she texted back.

And with a smile, she stood, and saw a pretty young woman with tasteful pink dreads and a nose ring, wearing violet scrubs, approach the brownstone.

"Heather?"

"Hi, Ivy."

Heather was an occupational therapist. Ivan had met her the day of his diagnosis. She'd suggested she could help him adjust to his declining health. She stopped by three days a week and spent about three or four hours with him. A big part of it was just providing companionship. But she did also assist him with things he had difficulty with like bathing and shaving.

"I don't believe you are scheduled for Mondays?"

"I'm not." She stopped on the bottom step. "My shift ended early and it's so close, I thought I'd stop by. I don't think Ivan will mind."

"Probably not. But we can't pay you for unscheduled visits."

"No problem, Ivy. I wouldn't expect it. I just like spending time with your brother."

Well. That was…exactly how she felt about Wolf. And Ivy wouldn't argue a friendship for her brother. She stood and opened the door and gestured that Heather enter. "Let's see what we can put together for lunch."

"I'm sorry," Wolf said after a sip of wine.

"No, I'm sorry," Ivy insisted from across the intimate table lit by flickering candlelight.

The waiter arrived to take their order. The restaurant was small, elegant, and located four steps below street level. It served amazing Korean barbecue that Wolf could eat by the bulk. But he'd rein in his voracious appetite because he didn't want Ivy to think him an oaf. Especially after their tense conversation earlier had resulted in her racing away from him.

The waiter left them with refills on their red wine.

When he was about to negate her need to apologize, Ivy put up a palm. So Wolf sat back. He wasn't a master at arguing with women. And he had the real scars to prove it. Best to hear her out.

"I reacted," Ivy said. "Your offer made me

feel…like you were trying to step in and take control."

"I would never—"

"I know. You're not that guy. So please, accept my apology. I don't often get in such a snit that I storm off from a conversation. I guess the unexpected offer caught me off guard."

He nodded. "Apology accepted."

"Never mention such an offer again."

He opened his mouth but then shut it. Never again? When his money might help them? And it would be like mere pennies to him. What was wrong with his money?

"Agreed?" she prompted.

Her sharp tone pinged at something inside Wolf. A stern warning about going against the rules. Or he would be overlooked. Forgotten. Forced into yet another home to be ruled over by yet another uncaring family that was only in it for the monthly support checks. Dispensable.

Wolf nodded silently, bowing his head. He didn't like to feel reprimanded. But he wasn't going to lash out at Ivy. She could have no idea how it made him feel. And he didn't want to make this little tiff even messier. Besides, he had begun to trust her, and that was a delicate thing he wanted to guard.

With an inhale, he set back his shoulders. "Then let's move forward. How was your day?"

"It was productive, actually. I found a possible insurance company and downloaded their information to read over the weekend. I also filled out an application for a medical research study that Ivan might qualify for."

"That's excellent. Is the research for a cure?"

"I don't know that a cure is so close on any medical front. It's for drugs that can arrest the disease from progressing."

"I don't know much about MS. Will you tell me about it?"

"I'm still learning myself. It's a central nervous system disease that disrupts blood flow and communication between the brain and the body. It can affect each person quite differently. Some can function in the real world without too many issues. Those in the middle are plagued by any number of symptoms like Ivan's fatigue, cognition issues, and muscle weakness. They can have periods of remission, then have sudden flare-ups. It's unpredictable. The worst, well, you'd mentioned you have a friend in a wheelchair. But it doesn't have to be a death sentence, by any means. Ivan just has to incorporate it into his life."

"That's gotta be tough for a man you said was intending to bike across the United States."

"Yes. Ivan has never not been active. He has good days and then there are days his hips hurt so badly he can't even get out of bed. I have hopes he won't digress to the level where he can't move on his own. Since I've moved in with him, he's been about the same. But that same is devastatingly inactive compared to his norm. It's quite humbling, actually."

"I know you don't want to hear this, Ivy." He wouldn't blow it again, but his heart wouldn't allow him to remain silent. "But I also need you to know…" He put his hand over hers. "I'm here for you. And your brother. It doesn't have to be monetary. Whatever you need, you've only to ask."

"That's kind of you." She clasped his hand. "Just having a friend who I can talk to means more than you can know."

"We are…friends." And how to change that? Did he want to? Things felt a little too unsure right now with Ivy. They clashed in ways that surprised him.

"Yes, but…"

"But?" Wolf looked up with hope prodding at his carefully protected heart. Perhaps he could prove a bit more indispensable to her than she thought?

At that moment the waiter arrived with their food.

Ivy quickly said, "Doesn't matter," then dove into her dinner.

Wolf wanted to know what that *but* had been about. Was the friend thing not working for her?

Did she want something more? She must understand that he needed to take it slowly with a woman. And yet, even as he had that thought, he knew what he had with Ivy had become more than a friendship. And that frightened him.

He cared about Ivy Quinn. And his heart was already deep in the thick of it.

Dare he make the leap and start to trust his own judgment? Did he really have to wait for the results of a background check? Even if something terrible were documented, he'd ignore it for the sake of his own needy want to be with her.

Was that it? He was needy when it came to love and affection. He'd a tendency to overlook a bad situation in hopes it might change. A welcome embrace was all he really needed. And it could happen with Ivy. If he took his time.

He raised his fork and said, "To the best damn barbecue in all of America."

"I'll give you that." She ate another bite and nodded in agreement. A hearty eater, she never shied from anything he offered her. About time he met a woman who didn't subsist on lettuce and diet soda. "You're originally from Germany?"

"Yes, Burghausen. In the western part of the country, not far from the Austrian border." At least, that's the only place he wanted to claim as his own. Heaven knew, he'd lived in too many places for any kid's sanity. "We're known for having the longest castle in the world. And there's the chemical factory. It's a pretty little village. You'd like it. Once you wander into the forested areas, there are plenty of bugs."

"I think I'd like any quaint little village. I'm all about traveling as soon as Ivan finds some stability. Then I hope to relocate overseas. Anywhere, really."

"It'll happen." He winked at her. "You are a smart woman, and I feel like nothing will stop you for long. You're just on a detour right now."

"A detour? In a coffee shop." Her shoulders dropped. "I am so not a barista."

"Yeah? But you make a mean cup of coffee. And I mean that literally. That stuff is so black it could wake a coma patient."

Ivy laughed. "That's about the only thing I can make. All those fancy lattes and frappes and espressos are silly. I still have to use the recipe cards to make some of them." She sighed. "People are really fierce about their drinks."

They shared tastes of their meals and Ivy liked his so he forked her a couple more pieces on the edge of her plate.

"I added a few classical songs to my playlist this morning on the walk to work," she said. "Did you like the concert?"

"I did! And I did the same. Working out to Beethoven's *Fifth* keeps the adrenaline pumping."

"Now if I see you in the gym when I walk by, I will immediately envision you lifting to Beethoven."

"I forget the gym is walled with windows. They used to have paper up on them. To keep the paparazzi from flocking."

"You must enjoy being able to walk around without having a camera snap your every move."

He shrugged.

"You like to be photographed?"

"I hate that. I snuck out of my place tonight and took a circuitous route here. Old habits. But what made them follow me was because I was dating someone. And… I guess I miss it."

"I thought you'd sworn off dating?"

"Yeah, but for the wrong reason. I do like the communication and companionship. Like what we have. I'm so glad you don't mind spending time with me, Ivy."

"Yes, well…" She shook her head and returned to eating. "It's not a hardship spending time with you. You're an interesting man. Despite our differences, we seem to work well together."

"We're not that different. We're both trying to survive in this crazy, busy world, dealing with whatever the universe decides to toss at us."

"Well, but you get to do that with a hefty bank

account. I'm not discounting that you earned it. I mean, you get tons of credit for building the Concierge empire from the ground up."

"I did have some excellent angel investors for the first few years."

"Because they knew you were worthy of such a risk. You're a true and genuine person, Wolf. I can only aspire to be like you someday."

Wolf winced. He didn't like to be put on a pedestal. Especially since he was not aspiration worthy. He'd led a tough life and had made plenty of mistakes along the way. The last one costing him a million dollars.

"Don't say that, Ivy. You'd never get taken to court for emotional distress."

She gaped at him. "Someone sued you?"

"My last girlfriend," he said. "Apparently, when a guy buys a diamond ring for a woman because she was swooning over the thing for ten minutes while we were shopping in Dubai, she takes it as a marriage proposal. I didn't even say the M word."

Ivy's jaw dropped open.

"I mean…" He studied her shock, unsure if it was because of what he'd done or what she would have expected. "Did I do the wrong thing? How would you have taken such a move?"

"I would have never begged for a diamond in the first place."

"Exactly. You're too classy. I got off easy, though. She started by asking for ten million. We settled for one."

"Just because she assumed the ring meant…? I can't believe some people. How long had you been dating?"

"Four weeks."

"Four— Did you love her?"

Had he been in love? Wolf wasn't sure what love felt like. He knew material things and sex did not equate to love. And yet, he had been soft on his last girlfriend. Perhaps even his heart had been open to a future with her.

"You must have been," Ivy decided. "I mean, to spend that much on a ring for her?"

He shrugged. "It was just a bauble. I like to give people things. It makes them happy."

He thought of his offer to pay for her brother's medical expenses. Damn. Maybe he had been trying to win her over with his money. Idiot.

"Doesn't matter because she got an even bigger payout with the lawsuit. She got to keep the ring, as well."

"Incredible. Now I really understand your reluctance to put yourself out on the dating scene again."

Wolf nodded, prodded at his food. It felt good to have spilled that to her. And yet, it also bothered him. Was he putting up another blockade to keep her from getting too close? Of course, he was! Yet, he wanted more with Ivy. Hell, he'd settle for a kiss. But he was skittish. And why did he have to be like that? He was a strong, capable man who had built his own empire.

Why the hell couldn't he just kiss the girl?

The waiter stopped by their table with the bill. He signed the receipt and added a fifty percent tip. Because the waiter had been courteous, and why the hell not?

Ivy sipped her wine and eyed him curiously.

"What? Do I have sauce on my beard?" He rubbed his chin. "You have to tell me if that happens. I can be a real ogre sometimes."

"I like the ogre in you. I looked something up last night."

"Yeah?"

"724717."

His genuine surprise manifested in a nodding grin as he swiped a hand over his beard. "That's *my* eye color?"

She nodded and waggled her shoulders, obviously proud of her sleuthing.

"Nice," he said. And about the most romantic thing a woman had ever done for him. Wow. Just, wow. "I'll have you speaking in code in no time."

"I like learning new things. What code is my shirt tonight?"

He studied the soft purple and said, "D9D2E9. It looks great on you. Goes well with your 74D4E7 eyes."

"Has anyone told you how romantic you are?" She batted her lashes at him. "Hey, that reminds me of that romance you are reading. Did you finish it?"

"I did, and I went back to the store for another one."

She leaned forward, this time her gape more wondrous. "Do tell."

"The author was Nora Roberts. The bookstore owner told me everyone reads her. It's about witches. I'm liking it."

Ivy sat back, her smile so delicious when she did that thing where she nodded her head and made her ponytail swing. That set his thoughts to pondering how he could accidentally unloose her hair and watch it spill over her shoulders. The guys in the romance novels did it all the time. Best to start taking notes as he read.

"I like you more every time we get together," she said. "I'm thankful for that calendar of yours."

"Me too. It was given to me by my best friend who is leaving for Sweden tomorrow. Used to be my director of operations."

"What's in Sweden?"

"A pretty woman with whom he wants to make a simple life. Much as he's been a backbone of Concierge, I didn't argue too much when he gave his notice."

"A simple life." She sipped her wine and wobbled the empty goblet before her. "That appeals to me. A little house in the country. A nice position with a solid research lab. Maybe a few kids later on in my thirties or even forties. A handsome husband who is happy with his work and…"

"And?"

She compressed her lips and he sensed she didn't want to say the next part out loud.

"Well," she offered with a conspiratorial lean across the table, "he has to believe in love. I don't think that's too much to ask."

No, it wasn't. Wolf wasn't sure he did believe in love. He had no idea how to define it. He was quite sure he'd never heard the words "I love you" in any of the foster homes in which he had grown up. And the few women he'd dated usually blurted it while he was handing them expensive gifts, so he'd never felt it a genuine statement of affection.

"What about you?" she prompted.

He couldn't tell her that he didn't believe in love.

"What kind of life do you enjoy?" she asked. "I suppose you thrive on the bustle of the big city and the techie job?"

Whew! He wouldn't have to reveal his cynical side tonight.

"Not at all. Confession? I moved to New York City because this was the place where I could grow Concierge. But now that it's established and we've got the next phase ready for release? I've begun thinking about what my next move is. I want to return to Germany."

"Interesting. I remember you saying something about too much concrete. The greenery in New York is rare, save for Central Park. So that village in Germany would make you happy? Was it the last place you were fostered?"

"No, it was the first place I moved after getting out of the foster care system. It's also where I started coding Concierge. It holds a lot of good memories for me. But I want to do it the right way."

Which, to Wolf, meant not going back alone. His idea of having made it? The wife and family. A fantasy he'd had since he was a kid who used to watch ancient reruns of family sitcoms.

"Space," Ivy idly said. "That's what you crave."

He could but nod in awe that she had accurately assessed his most basic and desperate desire. He really did crave a simple life. Space. It would come to him. But only if he had a supportive partner at his side.

Yet, that would never happen if he did not believe in love.

CHAPTER SEVEN

ON WEDNESDAY, Wolf had to examine his diet and make a positive change. He showed Ivy the calendar page. They both glanced to the slice of chocolate chip cake sitting before him. Both shook their heads.

"Absolutely not," he agreed with her laughter.

"Try drinking more water," she suggested. "It's supposed to be good for everything."

"Sounds much easier than sacrificing this," he said and took a big bite of the cake.

And yet, he knew the cake, while tasty, wasn't the reason he came to But First… every morning. And no calendar was going to stop that visit.

On Friday, Wolf stared at the calendar entry: *Do something unexpected*.

Following a quiet ping on his phone, he glanced to the text reminder on the Concierge app: Saturday office party.

Once a year, he threw a fancy black tie ball

for his employees, which included flying in the crew who worked remotely across the United States and France and a couple coders who lived in Germany. Everyone had a good time. Including himself.

Last year he'd brought a model who had been introduced to him at a tech conference. She'd seemed normal those first few dates. But following the Concierge party, the fireworks had exploded. And not the good kind of fireworks. She had left him with a literal scar on his bicep. He'd not dodged fast enough to avoid the knife she'd thrown at him. She'd been upset when he wouldn't agree to fund her shopping trip to Paris. He owed her after she'd spent a fortune on her gown for the party! When he'd laid down cash to cover the gown, she'd grabbed it, called him an asshole, and left, never to darken his threshold again.

Those disastrous relationships had scuttled his inner common sense. Could he ever trust his judgment if and when he actually found a genuine and real girlfriend?

When he'd given up on women six months ago, he'd only told Skyr. He hadn't suspected Skyr would gossip to the rest of the office, so he figured it had been Janice with her bionic ear. She occupied the office across the hallway from his.

This year, the entire office expected he'd show

up to the party alone. Janice couldn't hide the betting chart she had posted on what she thought was a secret online board. All office communications were monitored. Were they that naïve?

Flicking a glance to the desk calendar, he wondered what he could do that was unexpected. Everything he'd done since starting the calendar had been new and unexpected. Except the cold shower.

Janice popped her head into the office and waved the engraved invite for tomorrow's shindig. "I'm bringing a friend instead of my husband to the party. Is that okay?"

"Of course, it is. Plus-ones can be anybody, Janice."

"Thanks. Me and the hubby are not on good terms lately."

"I'm sorry to hear that." And really, stop there, he thought. Janice did like to unpack her personal stuff. To anyone who would listen.

"I think he's having an affair—"

He held up a hand to stop her. "I'm sorry, Janice. Take the friend. We'll be happy to have you both there."

"No plus-one for you, eh?" She winked.

Wolf controlled the wince and kept his mouth straight.

"Well, you know…" she started. With a dismissive wave of her hand, she then offered, "Nothing to worry about. We wouldn't expect our fearless leader to have to divide his time between master of ceremonies and a date. Bye!"

She quickly left.

And Wolf curled his fingers into fists. There was nothing wrong with showing up at his own party dateless. He was the fearless leader. A man who had to work the room, offer small talk with all the employees, smile at the plus-ones and seem interested in it all. It was a monumental task for a guy who preferred the solace of programming. But he understood the social side of business, and also genuinely liked to see his employees happy. It made for a successful work atmosphere.

He could bring a woman if he wanted to. She didn't have to be a girlfriend. She could just be a friend. Laugh, have a few drinks, take her home. Nothing like a date.

But why the hell *not* ask a woman out on a date? Hadn't he sacrificed long enough? He was seriously itching for a night with a woman, yes, laughing, having a few drinks, and then… maybe there would be more beyond that. Like sex. He loved sex. No-strings sex, especially.

He flicked a finger at the calendar and then leaned back in his chair. He could break his sabbatical. And it could be good. No fear of flying kitchen utensils. And wouldn't the office drop their jaws if he walked in with a woman? Janice would never reap the betting rewards.

He smirked. And then, nodded.

Wolfgang Zeigler could do whatever he damn well pleased. And he wanted to take a beautiful woman to the party.

Wolf walked into But First… with a big smile on his face. He laid the calendar page on the counter while Ivy filled his order. She picked it up and read it: "Do something unexpected?"

"Meet me at my corner table when you have a break?"

"Five minutes," she said.

Turning, Ivy walked right into Estelle, who wore the biggest grin on her face. "What?"

"You and that man finally getting cozy?"

"He's…" A very slow move. Her field journal had discovered his strengths and weaknesses. Dating was not a strength. "…just a friend, Estelle."

"Not according to that dreamy look you get in your eyes every time he sets foot in the café. Be careful, Ivy. If he's intent on playing the friend card, you will get hurt."

"I'm a big girl. I know what I'm doing. It's just…" Field notes? Please.

"All right. Carry on with your break. But I'll be watching him. You know I will."

"Wouldn't have it any other way." She grabbed the coffeepot and sailed over to Wolf's table. "Refill?"

"Half." He shoved his cup toward her and she filled half.

"So what's the unexpected?"

Setting his elbows on the table, he clasped his hands together and looked over them at her. Oh, those 724717s. "I have something to ask of you."

Sounded promising.

"Concierge is having our annual office party tomorrow night. It's black tie. At the Waldorf Astoria."

"I've heard about that place. It's a New York treasure."

"It is. And I was wondering if…you would like to go with me? On…a date?" he asked with a wincing lift of his shoulders.

"Seriously?" Yes! Calling all fire crews, the flames were getting higher! And yet… "What happened to taking a dating sabbatical?"

"Don't you want to go out with me?"

"Yes, I'd love to—I mean…" What had happened to focusing on Ivan? She lifted her chin. "Answer my question first. What's up?"

"Isn't asking you out unexpected?"

"It is. But if this is a real date, I don't want it to be a challenge date."

"I get that. I wanted to ask a beautiful woman

to the party, so I am. And I don't want it to be a friends thing. This is real. Can you deal with that?"

"I can deal." Ivan would be just fine for one night. "Can *you* deal?"

He smirked.

"I mean, what if I insist on sucking your bank account dry?"

"You wouldn't do that. But if you want to try, you can go for it."

"I would never."

"I know that about you." He winked. "So. What do you think? Are we…ready to move beyond friends?"

"More ready than you know," she said quickly before her common sense wrestled her inner romantic to the ground. "And it is very unexpected. Romantically burned bachelor asks temporary barista to a fancy party? Sounds like a romance novel."

"I do enjoy reading those. Another plus to this date is that it would also defeat Janice's betting pool about me showing up to the party dateless."

"Ah." Ivy set down the coffeepot. "We arrive at the real impetus behind your evil plan."

"It's—no. I mean, that's just a bonus. I'm not plotting anything evil—Ivy, I want to take you out. Show you a good time. Introduce you to the people I work with. Do date things. Like... kiss you?"

She raised a brow. All of the above sounded excellent. But she had to be sure this was more than just another challenge. Because her heart could not withstand any more teasing.

"Do you want me to beg?" he asked.

"Promise it will be a real date? Including the kiss?"

"Hell, yes."

"All right then. I would love to go on a date with you, Wolf. Tomorrow night?"

"Yes. This time, though, it's glamorous. You get to dress up. I'll do a black tie and fancy cuff links."

She owned nothing that would allow her to fit in with a black-tie crowd. But that wouldn't stop her from trying.

"I'll pick you up at eight," he said. "You're the only one I want to go to this party with me."

"I'll see you tomorrow night."

He thanked her and just when he spread his arms and it looked like he might move in for a hug, he adjusted his position and instead took her hand and shook it. "Thanks."

"Of course. So. Back to the grind. Literally!"

Ivy veered back behind the counter. She wanted to spill the details to Estelle, but the lunch crowd pouring in kept her busy for the next two hours. Only when the tables were wiped and the afternoon slump began was she able to punch out.

Estelle cornered her in the break room. "You've grown an inch since talking to Mr. Zeigler. What's going on with you two? And don't spare any of the salacious details."

"It's not salacious. It's…"

Dare she believe this was it, a real date? There were too many side factors that polluted the genuine date-ness of it. The office betting pool. The calendar challenge. The fact she'd not wanted to date a celebrity. Reservations abounded.

"I'm not going to explain. Suffice, he invited me to a fancy party tomorrow night and I have nothing to wear!"

"How fancy?"

"Waldorf Astoria fancy."

"Oh, sweetie, you need some help. And that hair."

"What about my hair?"

"It's always so…tight. You've got a day to get fancy party ready. You need a fairy godmother."

"Do you know where I can find one?"

Estelle called out Valerie's name and the slender Nigerian woman poked her head into the break room. "What up?"

Estelle studied Valerie, then switched her preening gaze to Ivy. Back and forth. "Valerie has a side job as a costume handler for a modeling agency, isn't that right?"

"It is. What do you need? Business suit? Afternoon tea dress with flounces and fascinator? Thigh boots and leather bodysuit?"

"A ball gown," Estelle declared, with a flourishing gesture toward Ivy.

Valerie eyed up Ivy, who now felt like a piece of meat on display at the grocer. Then she nodded. "I have something perfect. But what about her hair?"

"Exactly." Estelle put her hands akimbo and said to Ivy, "One fairy godmother coming right up!"

A manila envelope lay on Wolf's desk. His name was typed on a white sticker affixed to the upper right corner. A scan of the QR code below indicated it was from the private investigator.

He turned the envelope over and pushed his forefinger under the flap, then…stopped. Frowning, he decided to open a drawer and drop the envelope inside. Whatever the PI had learned about Ivy could wait. He'd already asked her to the party. If there was damning info inside the envelope, it was too late to cancel.

And he didn't want to cancel. He wanted to take Ivy out on a real date. For himself.

He'd open it later. Maybe.

CHAPTER EIGHT

IVY COULD NOT believe her luck. The gush of frothy red fabric that billowed out of the dress bag made her do a little dance, hands to her mouth. And she actually squealed.

"Are you serious?" she asked Valerie, who fluffed out the gorgeous creation she'd just revealed.

Estelle walked around the dress, nodding in appreciation. "This one belongs on a princess." She glanced at Ivy. "I guess I really am your fairy godmother."

"I can't believe this. Are you sure it's okay to borrow it? It's so fabulous. And it looks spendy."

Valerie laid the dress across Ivy's white comforter. The bedroom was ultra-modern, all white and pale pine so the red screamed. "It is spendy. And it is fabulous. We used this on a Vogue shoot. It's due back at the designer on Monday. That means I need it back tomorrow."

"Or you'll turn into a pumpkin," Estelle added with a laugh.

"Do you have glass slippers, too?" Ivy asked as she ran her palm over the soft, floaty material.

"Will Louboutins do?" Valerie pulled out a shoe box from her bag.

"Are you kidding me?" Ivy sat and took it in, gliding a hand over the tulle fabric. Never in her wildest dreams had she imagined Valerie would bring something so beautiful. And expensive. And, yes, worthy of a princess. "I can't wear it. What if I spill on it?"

"You will not spill on it," Valerie admonished tersely. "Or I will get stuck with the cleaning bill. It's okay, Ivy. This dress was made for your figure. It looks fluffy but it's sturdy. Don't you want to try it on?"

"Yes!"

"I'll get the curling iron," Estelle said, heading toward the makeup bag she'd toted along. "We're going to make a princess out of you tonight!"

Wolf adjusted his tie before the mirror. Suits were uncomfortable. He rarely wore them. But the black-tie party made the event more special. Anticipation always shimmered through the office. An excuse to buy a new dress for some. And hell, the men liked to look dapper, too.

"Dapper?" He peered suspiciously at his reflection. "How old are you? Keep it together, man. Tonight will be fun."

And that Ivy had said yes to a date that wasn't between friends? Score! But caution must be wielded. She didn't look at him with dollar bills in her eyes. Hell, she'd been upset by his spur-of-the-moment offer to help pay her brother's medical bills. But a guy just never knew. The armor that wrapped his heart was solid.

As well, everyone would see he had a girlfriend and they could all stop gossiping behind his back. And they would also stop trying to fix him up. If Ellen in sales stopped by one more time to show him a photo of her cousin or niece or long-lost sister…

He flicked off the lights and tucked his phone in a pocket before heading down the hallway to the elevator.

Twenty minutes later, the limo pulled up before Ivy's building. It was an older brownstone walk-up with masses of climbing greenery covering the façade and a gothic iron fence. Ivan had scored well with this house-sitting job. And he got to stay in the place for almost a year? The guy was industrious, as well as smart.

"I'll head up," Wolf said to the driver. "Shouldn't take long."

He got out of the back seat just as an incredible vision floated through the front door to stand at the top of the steps. A princess in candy red. A fitted bodice accentuated her gorgeous bust and slender waist. From there the skirt blossomed out in waves of red, dusting the steps in froths of ruffle. It was as if a lush treat stood waiting for him to dive in, swim and lose himself. And her hair, no longer tidied in a ponytail, spilled over a shoulder and down her arm in sleek curves.

But that wasn't what took his breath away. Her lips matched her dress. Perfect bow lips that parted slightly when she noticed him standing before the limo.

"F80825," he whispered. He could practically smell the bright, delicious color. And taste her kiss.

All of a sudden her eyes brightened and her smile felt like a warm beam of happiness to his heart.

Wolf exhaled. He'd not expected a date with a princess this evening. Hell, he should have spent more time with his grooming rather than finger-combing his hair after a shower and smacking on a bit of beard oil. And had he remembered deodorant? He'd forgotten cologne! Would she notice? Would she flinch when she felt the touch of his sweaty hands?

Get it together, man!

"Hey!" She waved, then gathered up her skirt to carefully ascend the few steps. When she landed on the sidewalk, she twirled, swishing the skirt out in a wide, billowing circle. "What do you think? Good enough for the Waldorf?"

Good enough? Ivy Quinn was beyond. The Waldorf was not good enough for her. This woman belonged on a pedestal so that others could gaze up and adore her like the princess she was.

"Wolf?" She peered at him carefully. "Is everything okay? It's too much, isn't it? Oh, I—"

"It's perfect." He caught her hand in a clasp and pulled her closer to him. She smelled like flowers and her eyelids glinted with sparkles. Her mouth pursed. And he wanted to touch every part of her, taste her…

What do you think you're going to do, Zeigler? Kiss the girl?

If he was lucky? Yes. Tonight was a beginning. *To everything.* He hoped it would go well.

"A friend lent it to me." She slipped her hand from his and fluffed at the skirt. "Because seriously? I don't have something so fabulous as this just hanging in my closet. You look very handsome. Dapper."

Wolf laughed at the word she used.

"What? You don't think so?"

He leaned in and kissed her cheek. A reaction.

He'd kissed the princess! Now, to not mess up the rest of the night so he could earn a real kiss on her lips.

"You look incredible, Ivy. I can't believe I get to escort such a beautiful woman tonight. All eyes will be on you." He hooked his arm for her to take. "Let's do this."

As the limo cruised through Manhattan, slowly making its way to the Waldorf Astoria, Ivy got a handle on her nerves and was able to relax against the seat. Until she thought of something. Her shoulders tightened.

"What's our story?" she suddenly asked Wolf.

"Our story?"

"I know this is all for your challenge calendar, but for your employees' sake, is this our first date? What does the office think? You mentioned something about quelling some rumors, so I feel like I have to be on my toes. Have we been dating? How long?"

"Ivy, chill. It's our first date. Of a sort. I kind of count the orchestra as a date too."

So he did consider this a real date? But also a challenge.

"I...do, too." But there hadn't been a kiss, so... Not a real first date by her standards. "Right then." She smoothed her palms over the red fabric, using the motion to focus and deflect her annoying nerves. "Just chill. And yet...all the people will be staring at us because the boss who swore off dating is there with someone."

He chuckled in that deep tone that snapped at her nerves and teased up a soft, sensual relaxation of her muscles. "They have a habit of keeping an eye on me."

"That's sweet in a weird stalker-ish way."

"Are you nervous?"

"Of course!"

"I am, too."

"You are? Why?"

"Because look at you. You're...everything."

The hush on the word *everything* settled at the base of her throat and felt as much like a kiss as she could imagine. Ivy closed her eyes and nodded. This really was a fantasy night. And she intended to enjoy every moment of it.

"You don't think I'm overwhelmed to be sitting in a limo with the handsomest man I've ever fed cake to?" she asked.

He turned on the seat to face her and she tried not to make direct eye contact. Too intense. Most importantly, she didn't want to sweat in this dress!

Focus on enjoying yourself!

"Relax, Ivy. Everyone is going to love you."

With an accepting nod, she looked out the window at the passing shop fronts. He saw her as different from the other women he'd dated, and whom he had decided were terrible. That was good, right?

Ivy wasn't sure, exactly, what sort of woman would appeal to Wolfgang Zeigler. And much as this was a date, this was also just another page to tick off for his calendar challenge. It was a weird situation to be wearing a fantasy gown and walking into a fabulous party on the arm of a man who had already conjured many a late-night sex dream.

Then again, who didn't dream about a man before their official date? It was a prelude to what she hoped would come true. Tonight? She wanted to get that kiss for sure.

"We are here, Mr. Zeigler," the driver announced.

"Thanks, Charles." Wolf grinned at Ivy. Touched her lower lip with his thumb.

"How's my lipstick?" she asked.

"Perfect. F80825." His eyes wandered over her lips, and then finally up to her eyes, as if he'd gotten lost. He blew out a breath. "I really want to kiss you."

Yes! Heartbeat racing, she managed, "Same."

He clasped her hand and kissed the side of it. "But not right here. Are you ready?"

For the forthcoming kiss? Hell, yes! But she

knew he meant to walk inside on his arm. To fully commit to the fantasy.

"Ready as I'll ever be."

The Waldorf Astoria on Park Avenue was *the* place in New York for glamour, riches, and celebrations. Sure, it was a bit old-school, but Wolf tended toward the less modern and trendy. Some of his best memories of Germany were while living in a town known for its castles; of course, he preferred the grandeur and pomp of things.

The grand ballroom had been recently remodeled. The Art Deco space had been restored to its early splendor. Wolf's eyes slid along the elegant gilded ceiling reliefs and the walls. Two tiers of balconies overlooked the dance floor and a couple employees in them waved as they sighted him. Concierge employed about three hundred people worldwide. And tonight he intended to treat them to a sumptuous party.

"Wolf!"

He waved to a couple who acknowledged him with a lift of their champagne goblets. Ivy held his hand a little tighter. The woman certainly had daring to walk into this situation. Three paparazzi had manned the curb as they'd arrived. They'd snapped some shots, much to Ivy's surprise. He'd quickly guided her inside, fighting the urge to yell at them to get the hell away. How did they know when to seek him out? Only an employee could have given them info about tonight's party. Or a hotel employee. He'd thought he'd paid enough for privacy, but apparently not. But the press weren't allowed access to the ballroom, so this was a safe zone.

"How you doing?" he asked Ivy.

"Overwhelmed after our exit from the car but now…excited. Let's get some champagne in me and make things a little easier."

"I like how you think."

Ivy had been introduced to dozens of people. All shook her hand and commented on her dress. They were friendly, all seemed in awe of their fearless leader, and most whispered as she walked away on Wolf's arm. Wondering if the boss's new fling would hurt him as so many others had before her?

Ivy had no intention of hurting Wolf. And she couldn't understand the mindset of a person who would demand things and expect money from a person just because they had so much.

Earlier, Wolf had whispered a warning not to talk too long to Janice because she'd learn her life story. So when she approached now, Ivy braced herself. Instead of shaking Ivy's hand, the woman leaned in for a buss of both cheeks. Weirdly awkward, and she pulled back with a greedy smile on her face. "You're so beautiful. And quite…unexpected."

Ivy flashed a smile to Wolf at the use of that word. He shrugged and then took her hand. "We need to make the rounds," he said apologetically to Janice, then whisked her away.

"Catch you later!" Janice called with a wave and a discerning cast of what felt to Ivy like the evil eye.

"Was I right?" Wolf asked.

"She does give me a weird stalker vibe."

"She's not that extreme, but there are days when I wonder if there's a listening device from her office directly to mine. There's a couple employees from the overseas offices. Let's go say hi."

As they did, the band kicked into an anthem rock song and the crowd applauded. Champagne glasses were raised. The dance floor filled. And Ivy floated through the dream alongside her Prince Charming.

A few hours into the party, Ivy and Wolf had drifted apart, which was fine with her. He needed to work the room, and she had stolen a moment to slip into the bathroom and inspect her hair and lipstick.

The lip stain Valerie had lent her really did stay on. What was the code for it? She couldn't recall, but she marveled that Wolf must see colors as numbers. A weird bit of synesthesia brought on by his years of coding? It was a quirk that made her feel as if she were privy to a secret part of him that others may never understand.

"Oh, Ivy." A woman in a glittery white gown cut low to reveal a star tattoo on one of her breasts sidled up alongside Ivy before the marble vanity. She seemed about Ivy's age, perhaps even late twenties. The glitter in her hair was subtle, glamourous. "I'm Sandra. We haven't met but everyone is whispering your name. The gorgeous model on Wolf's arm."

"Oh, I'm not a—"

"I know. An entomologist? Janice told me. She's been gathering intel about you."

Ivy cautioned herself from rolling her eyes at that information.

"Where did the two of you ever find each other?"

"At the coffee shop on the first floor of his building."

"But First…? Oh. Huh." The woman studied Ivy's reflection more carefully. "Maybe I have seen you before… So, you're just a barista?"

The last thing she wanted was for the office gossip to whisper that Wolf was dating a barista. Not cool for a man of his clout.

"It's a temporary job until I begin work with

an institute later this year," she lied. Wishful thinking? More like a form of protection for Wolf's reputation. "That dress is beautiful."

"Oh, thanks. I love this party! It's the only opportunity I get to dress up and play at princess."

"I can relate. My fairy godmother fixed me up with this dress."

"She certainly knows your color. That red. Well, you're gorgeous. You just be nice to our Wolf, okay?"

"I…uh…of course. I wouldn't be anything but."

"Well." Ivy felt the woman's gaze switch to judgmental in a snap. "He's a good man. Too good. We'll be keeping an eye on you." With that, the woman left the bathroom.

"They really care about their boss," she muttered.

A good thing. More often than not, employees tended to despise their boss. Wolf was a kind man. Who had obviously been hurt in his relationships.

Did she actually think she could be the woman to change that?

"Not if I can't break through his emotional barriers."

And hers as well. She'd been shocked by the paparazzi flashes upon entering. Had cringed. And for a moment had felt like climbing back into the limo and hiding. She'd thought dating a celebrity was not for her. And having gotten a taste of it, did she really believe she could manage the loss of privacy? And what if they learned about her brother? She had to protect Ivan from it all. He did not need that added stress right now.

This couldn't go on. She had too much to protect. Perhaps tonight was merely meant to be one fantasy night to remember. A treat. And then back to real life.

CHAPTER NINE

WOLF CLOSED HIS eyes and leaned against the wall. He'd found a cove away from the main ballroom. He'd schmoozed and laughed, and smiled, and chatted. An escape was necessary to recharge his battery. He was thankful this was a once-yearly party. But he was glad to see all his employees so happy. And he'd not met a few of the international associates, beyond Zoom, so that had been great to finally shake hands and chat.

With an empty beer mug dangling from one hand, he remembered Ivy had spoken the word *space*, and it made him smile. Yes, she understood that part of him he guarded so fiercely.

Everyone had come up to him and told him they liked Ivy, that she was beautiful, and interesting. He'd found a good one. Now the office gossip would cease. Or would it only get fueled? Surely the paparazzi would label her his girlfriend in whatever media they posted those photos. This was a date, after all. And yet…

Could he do that to Ivy? Thrust her in the path of the hungry photogs merely because he enjoyed spending time with her?

Ivy was incredible. Not only was she gorgeous, outgoing, and so easy to be with, she seemed to sense when he was open to her being at his side and also when he needed a squeeze from her hand.

He'd kissed that hand a few times as they'd navigated from small chat to small chat. Man, he wanted to give her a real kiss. To linger in the discovery of her soft mouth, her scent, the lithe and responsive curves of her body. He could take her home with him... No, he couldn't expect her to go beyond a kiss on the first date. Could he? Happened all the time with his previous girlfriends.

Maybe there was something to that. If he'd gone slower with those women, gotten to know them before moving right to sex, would the course of those relationships have gone differently? Been more trusting?

He did enjoy the companionship. And he did enjoy sex. And he did enjoy Ivy. Dare he tell her as much? Would that ruin her expectations of him? This was supposed to be a fun evening, just another challenge presented by that stupid calendar. That it gave him such conflicting emotions about everything was enough to make him want to toss the thing in the trash when he got back to the office.

"Hey, there you are." Ivy walked up and put her back to the wall to stand beside him. "Mind if I hide out with you? They've turned up the music and everyone is shaking their booties."

"You don't shake your booty?"

"I do, but I'm afraid this dress is a little too delicate for that hip-hop action going on out there."

"Then do join me. I needed to escape. It's an introvert thing."

"I get it."

"You do. Which is surprising to me. Usually extroverts can't comprehend our brains."

"I'll give you that. But I did date an introvert a few years ago. That taught me some people are not wired for exuberant conversations. They need to recharge their batteries. I'm good with it. Even we extroverts need the occasional recharge."

"Bless you."

She tilted her head onto his shoulder. "Thank you for inviting me tonight. It's been a lot of fun. A much-needed release from life's worries."

"How is your brother?"

"He invited Heather over to watch a movie with him. I had intended to not think about him tonight. You know, just try to enjoy the evening."

"Sorry, I shouldn't have brought it up."

"It's fine. I know you care."

"I do, Ivy. I really do." He clasped her hand and kissed the back of it. "You know there will be more paparazzi waiting for us to leave?"

"I suspect so. That was…eye-opening. I can't imagine living a life where you have to always be concerned about others intruding on your every moment."

"It's why my dating life is a shambles. But I think the reward is worth the risk. At least, with you."

"Really? You'd forge through hordes of reporters just for me?"

"I would. But I really shouldn't ask the same of you. It's tough for someone who has never experienced it before."

"It is interesting. I hope I don't make Page Six."

"Are you regretting going out with me tonight?"

"Honestly? Yes and no. Yes, to the photogs. No, to spending time with you."

"So…uh…" He leaned forward, his eyes dancing with hers. "We are alone."

Ivy bowed her head, looking up through her lashes at Wolf.

He slipped his hand along her neck. The electric connection skittered down her spine, opening her like a flower. As his hand glided up through her hair, feeding that vibrant shock of desire, she closed her eyes as his lips touched hers.

Heat. Power. Passion. It mingled, creating an intense moment of connection. Wolf's breath danced with hers. Her skin shimmied in a tingling sensation. Champagne and body heat and a certain masculine perfume surrounded her.

Ivy could have never anticipated this moment. Standing in a fancy ballroom, wearing a princess dress, being kissed by the man who held a place in her dreams. And, oh, what a kiss.

Body curving forward, her bones went liquid, seeking Wolf's brute physicality. Melding against him, she gave him every sigh, every wish that she'd had about him. His mouth explored hers, knowing exactly how to touch, with firm pressure yet a soft teasing tongue. Fingers twined into her hair, holding her to him, keeping her. Making her his.

I am yours. For tonight.

With heartbeats racing, she gripped at his suit lapels, twisting, taking from him. The dress hem was so fluffy their feet didn't meet, but their hips did. He wanted her. She wanted him. Could she climb inside him and live there? Away from the world? Away from everything that could ever challenge or give her pain? What a dream.

Ending the kiss with a slow parting, they bowed

their foreheads together. Ivy had never felt a kiss so perfectly easy and yet electrically exciting. She wanted another.

Dipping her head, she kissed his mouth, hot from their connection. He tasted salty and calm. Sparks of champagne mingled with the masculine heat of him. The brush of his beard and mustache teased her nipples to peaks.

His eyes danced over her face. "I've never felt a kiss like I just did."

"Same."

He kissed her cheek and thumbed her jaw before brushing the hair from her face. "You told me you felt like a princess tonight."

"Well, come on, I've got the dress, the shoes, a fairy godmother who sent me off. I'm not sure if I'll turn into a pile of rags before the stroke of midnight, though. We should be very careful the limo doesn't shapeshift into a pumpkin on the ride home."

He laughed and kissed her forehead. "I'll protect my princess. But why is it the women always get the fairy-tale dreams? We aspiring princes have our fantasies, too."

"White stallions and vanquishing swords?"

He smirked and bowed his head before looking up into her eyes. "I was thinking more along the lines of being seen and accepted."

Those simple dreams grabbed Ivy by the

heart and squeezed, gently, but enough to make her mush from the tips of her lashes to her toes.

"I see you," she said.

"I know that you do. It's...humbling."

She hugged him. And he hugged her back. If that was all it took for the man's dreams to be fulfilled then her part was easy.

Never had she hugged a person for so long. Really let her body melt against his, feel his presence, his warmth, his very being. It felt beyond good. And not even in a sexual way. They connected on a DNA level that she had once read about in college. When humans touched they actually shared vulnerabilities, respect, and could even promote healing. Actual RNA was also shared. It was amazing.

Wolf was the one to pull away and kiss her quickly before saying, "That's the best hug I've ever had."

"Almost better than the kiss."

"Promise me that wasn't our last?"

Could she make such a promise? The paparazzi's insistent flashes had warned her to be more cautious. What to say that wouldn't disappoint him?

"Wolf!"

They turned to find someone waving his drink high and gesturing toward the ballroom. "Speech?"

"I'd better go and thank them all," Wolf said. He kissed her hand. "This has been the best night."

The limo parked before Ivy's building. She'd had a night! It was sad that it had come to an end, but she was thoroughly exhausted and almost glad for the finale. Almost. Leaving Wolf's embrace felt unimaginable. Yet, the stumble through a barrage of paparazzi to the limo had further cemented her determination to make this a one-night experience.

"Thank you," he said, clasping her hand.

"Anything to help you out with your challenges," she offered, trying to make light of something she'd fallen deep into and wasn't sure how to climb out of.

"Ivy, don't do that. Do you think tonight was just for the calendar? It wasn't. Please tell me you know that."

The desperation in his tone chided her. Why did she have to insist on keeping them at a distance even after that kiss? Oh, that kiss!

"Of course, I know it was a real date. I was just teasing." But if she was truthful with herself, it had been a form of protection against her already challenged emotional reserves. Amazing kiss or not, she had to draw a line. "Don't even tell me if my face shows up on the socials tomorrow, okay?"

"I won't. Promise." He kissed her hand. "Did you have a good time?"

"I did. It was like a fairy tale." A once-in-a-lifetime adventure. "And speaking of tales of wonder, I have to get this dress back to my friend tomorrow or else she'll send the cavalry after me."

Wolf laughed. Then he stroked her hair. "I like your hair down. It's so soft."

"Being a barista is not glamorous. If I don't tie my hair back, it'll end up in someone's coffee. But it was fun to go glamorous tonight. Now, as soon as I leave this coach, it will turn into a pumpkin." She opened the back door, pushed to get out, and then turned to smile at him.

The kiss was unavoidable. Her field note journal abandoned for real experience. Had she thought to capture this man in her net? Because really, there were thousands of butterflies fluttering throughout her system with his kiss. And they were captured within, free to react to Wolf's every sensual touch. She had to escape his net before it was too late.

He bowed his forehead to hers. "I'd ask to come inside, but I wouldn't be at all surprised if your brother was waiting by the door. Do you have a curfew?"

"Nope. But I won't invite you in. The place is very open. There's not a lot of privacy."

"I get it. We could have gone to my place…"

Was he intimating they might have ended the night in bed? Ivy could certainly get behind that. Or rather, in between those sheets.

And yet, with her official dating badge so shiny and new, she was reluctant to crawl into bed with Wolf. Sex meant something to her. She didn't have flings or share her body with just anyone. Emotions were involved and she required, at the very least, the suggestion of a commitment before she got naked with a man. And above all, no paparazzi to record the event.

"Maybe," she said in response to the open-ended sort of suggestion. "But I really should be getting inside. I don't like to leave Ivan alone too long. He has trouble getting into bed sometimes. I should go in and check on him."

And avoid the gorilla sitting on the trunk behind them? The will-they-won't-they? Their kiss seemed to want to lead somewhere, but not into bed.

"I get it," he said.

No, he really didn't, because even she couldn't get things straight in her brain right now.

"I've got an early morning at the office."

He always did. Why couldn't she just grab him by the collar and shake some honesty out of him? Make him face the truth? Make him commit to either being in or out with her? Again, it was those boundaries of his. She didn't want to break them and risk him fleeing. He was too precious to her. And she knew that men could be vulnerable when pressed.

And really, what did she expect? The night had come to an end. She had to move forward, away from the drama that surrounded Wolf's life.

"To a fairy-tale night," she said, then gave him a quick kiss. "See you in the morning?"

"Always."

She left him sitting inside the limo. Once inside she saw that Ivan's bedroom light was off. A quick peek confirmed he was asleep. All was well.

Except with her heart.

Wolf blew out a breath and stretched his arms across the back of the limo. He'd almost suggested they go back to his place and have sex. Ivy had successfully dodged that unspoken prompt. He'd give her the benefit of the doubt. Her brother did need care.

What was he doing? He hadn't needed to impress anyone tonight. Hadn't needed to prove to his employees that he was happily dating to stop the rumors. So why couldn't he just step out of the role and be himself? The man who wanted Ivy more and more. A man who felt as though a piece of him were missing when she was not around.

CHAPTER TEN

IVY HANDED VALERIE the dress bag and the shoe-box. She had intended to deliver the dress to her this morning but Valerie, who currently stood in the living room, said it had been no problem to stop by. Which meant, she had been nervous about its safe return.

"Thank you again," Ivy said. "It made the night like something out of a fairy tale."

"Oh, I think it was the handsome prince you were seen smooching in the limo that did that," Valerie said.

Ivy gaped.

"Page Six, my dear." The side glance Valerie gave her, accompanied with a smirk said everything Ivy needed to know. "I'll see you at work tomorrow."

Ivy's heart sank. She'd been photographed while kissing Wolf? Must have been as they'd left the party. Yes, he had given her a smooch in the back of the car. She'd been so enthralled by him, she hadn't realized the paparazzi had surrounded the car until the limo driver had apologized for his slow departure as he had to carefully navigate the throngs.

Tugging out her phone, she almost typed in Page Six, then shook her head. "Don't do it."

But curiosity prodded. The page came up, and there she and Wolf were in a huge photo in the back of the limo. They weren't kissing, but he was leaning in looking like he might be kissing her. It had really been that he'd been reaching to shield the flashes with his hand out her side of the vehicle.

The headline read: *Billionaire Rogue Romeo Seen with Mystery Woman.*

And underneath:

Creator of Concierge app back on the dating scene. Who is the mystery woman in red? And how much will she take him for?

"Really? Those assholes."

They'd taken a perfectly romantic first date and made it wrong. Already labeling her a gold digger? The nerve!

Ivy swore under her breath just as Ivan walked into the kitchen. He was quite steady and didn't use the cane any more than to direct his steps.

"The woman in red," he said and winked. "Oh, sister, what have you gotten into?"

"I'm not sure. This is terrible."

"You're not dating Wolf?"

"Well, yes, it was a date. But look, this ridiculous article claims I'm going to take him for another million like his former girlfriend did. How dare they!"

"It's what those vultures do. Sensationalism sells much better than 'it's their first date and they were so precious.'"

"What a mess." She slammed her phone down on the counter. She'd not wanted to involve Ivan in any sort of gossip. He had enough stress to deal with. If she continued to see Wolf, would the paparazzi follow her home?

"Well, I think you two look great together. Don't you want it to be a thing?"

"I've got too much on my plate to think about having a relationship, Ivan."

"Are you talking about me? Because I will not be used as an excuse to avoid your own personal issues."

"Yes, but... I don't want it to affect you. You've got enough on your plate right now."

He shrugged. "We'll deal with that if it happens. From the little you've told me, Wolf seems like a nice guy. Dude is rich, too. What's not to like about him?"

"I tend to look beyond a person's financial worth. I'm surprised you'd even say such a thing."

"I'm sorry. I know you do. As do I. But how can you not entertain thoughts about all his cash? He's swimming in money."

"I like Wolf for who he is. And I hope he likes me for who I am."

"Does he know you're not a coffee slinger in real life?"

"Yes, and he's afraid of spiders."

"The horror!" Ivan sighed and shrugged. "That man will never be the one for you. If a little bug scares him…"

Ivy stuck out her tongue at him. But he wasn't wrong. Had she netted a catch that was too big even for her to handle? But where *did* she stand after their first official date? True, she should not use Ivan's health as an excuse to avoid a relationship. And he'd brushed it off as insignificant. But after she helped her brother get his life settled, she intended to find a real job, possibly not even on this continent. Where would that leave her future with Wolf?

On Monday, Wolf met Ivy outside But First… She handed him a cup of black coffee, and then gave him a bite of her chocolate-frosted donut.

"Not so big!" she protested when he took a chunk out of one side and handed it back to her.

"Yeesh, it's like you've never seen food every time you see food. Have you eaten lunch?"

"Today?"

She rolled her eyes, and took a bite of the donut, then handed the rest to him. "Have at it. It was just a treat. But you need fuel to keep that brain working properly."

He downed the donut in two bites as they walked. "You think sugar is good fuel for thinking?"

"Not really. But at least the calories will go to your hips instead of mine."

He leaned in and gave her a kiss that tasted like chocolate and donut crumbs.

"I can get behind those invisible calories," she said. "Kiss me again?"

They paused and just when she was prepared to meet his mouth with hers, he took a moment to glance over her shoulder.

"What? Paparazzi?"

"Surprisingly? Not one in sight. Which makes me nervous. They could be hiding, getting long-range shots. Let's keep walking."

Disturbed that they could be followed, Ivy shifted her focus. Was she moving forward in this relationship? It felt like it. And honestly, she wanted to explore their connection. Her heart was screaming to give it a chance. Was there a way to make it happen while also protecting Ivan from the nosy press?

"I've got a meeting in half an hour so this will have to be a quick walk."

She nodded and sipped her coffee. "What does a day in Wolf Zeigler's life look like?"

"At Concierge? Boss things. Coding, for sure. But I have dozens of excellent coders on staff, here and in Europe. So I've been able to let some of my work be divvied out to them. I oversee all the designs and tech on the new apps. We have two planned for release next year, which is what the meeting is about."

"Can you tell me what they are?"

"Sure, but then I'd have to kill you. And I don't think I'm cut out for burying a body."

"But the killing part works for you?"

Wolf laughed. "Touché. I'll give you a hint: it involves NFTs and creating an accessible marketplace."

"NFTs. Non-fungible tokens," she said. "And that's all I know about that."

"You got the acronym right. That's better than ninety percent of non-techies. I'm also teasing the idea of selling Concierge. The app, that is."

"But doesn't it make you tons of money?"

"It does. And I would probably make a cool billion selling it."

"Why sell when you can continue the income stream?"

They paused beneath a flowering tree. Wolf turned to her, crushing his empty coffee cup. She did not miss his scan of the neighborhood. Being protective? Mark another one off her list. And yet, she really wished they'd stayed indoors, away from spying cameras.

"Ivy, I don't need more money. I have more money than God. In fact, I don't think God has money. That would just be wrong. Anyway, I'm set for life. So I want to start focusing on what comes next. My life."

"Your life? You don't have one now?"

"Do you think spending sixteen hours a day at work is a life?"

"Not at all. So what's next?"

"Well—you gave me an idea."

"I did?"

"Yes, you've inspired me to start investigating charities and design a plan for distributing my income. I figure giving half away should be good for starters."

"That's a hell of a lot of money. But also, that's amazing. How did I inspire such a grand idea?"

"When you told me about your brother, I started thinking about ways I could help people. You know, people that would take the help."

She got the dig. And she still wasn't changing her mind regarding taking financial help from him. "Good for you. What focus are you going for? Humanities? Environmental? Technological?"

"All of the above? I'm not sure yet. I'm just getting this idea going. I alerted my financial advisor. And you know? It's already made me feel lighter. Like all this money will become much less of a burden than it's been to me."

"The burden landing squarely on your failed relationships?"

"Yes."

"Are you sure it's all because of your money? Maybe it's you?"

"Well, hell, I'm such a lovable guy, it's got to be the money, right?"

She caught his wink and laughed. "All right, I concede. You are a lovable guy. And any woman who can't see beyond your dollar signs is crazy."

"You've seen beyond the dollars."

"Because you let me. But seeing beyond all those camera flashes the other night was a challenge." And now would be the perfect time to tell him about her hesitancy...

"I hate that others have to suffer just because they want to spend time with me. If I could pay them all to stay away from me, I would." He made another surveillance around them. "But the money would just make them even more greedy. Blackmail involved, I'm sure. I'd hand it all back for some peace, trust me on that one. And...for a simple, quiet life."

"Really? I have to believe that you'd keep some of it. Just enough to make that simple quiet life?"

"Yeah, you're right. A little cottage out in the woods and a family are on my radar."

"Wow, that does surprise me. Do you think it's even possible?"

"Escaping the paparazzi can be done. Especially when they think they are being covert. Three o'clock in the bushes. See that lens?"

Ivy twisted her glance to the right. Sunlight flashed in the middle of a hedge. Mercy. "I have to tell you that I'm a little worried about them."

"The paps? Don't be. I'll protect you from them. Promise."

"I know you will, and that's not the part that scares me." Now that she'd seen the paparazzi, she couldn't look away. "It's Ivan. If we, well... the more we're seen together and photos are taken, then they'll probably look into me and my life. I don't want any of this craziness to carry back to my brother. He doesn't need that."

"I get it. But I can't protect your brother from what they write. Or you. That headline was nasty. You're not a gold digger. I know that. You just have to not read anything they write."

"Easier said than done. I know it's not your fault what the press prints. I just had to tell you that so you know where I stand. Because, well, I know last night was a date. But what does that mean? Are we dating now? Are we…"

"I've been thinking about that, too. Ever since I watched you walk up to the brownstone and close the door, I wanted to be inside that house with you. Not standing outside."

"Same."

"Really?"

"Yes. Wolf, I know how you feel about dating, and believe me, I respect your need to be cautious and go slow. However—"

He leaned in and kissed her. It was a kiss she had been waiting for all her life. A real one. An honest one. One that said they shared things, understood one another. But it ended too abruptly. And she followed his glance across the street to the jiggling shrubbery.

"We've gone slow," he said. "I trust you, Ivy. I know you're not interested in my money."

"I'm not."

"Are you interested in me?"

"Hell, yes. But I wouldn't have invited you in last night, brother or not. I'm not the sort who gets intimate with a man unless we're exclusive. Sex is special to me."

"I'm glad you told me that. I want you to be

my girlfriend. And not because I think there will be sex sometime in the future. I want the exclusivity thing, too. We're more than friends. Do you think you can handle dating a reclusive introvert with a penchant for eating too much and with more money than he knows how to spend?"

"He sounds a little quirky," she said.

"And there is the added hindrance of spying your every intimate moment on all the socials."

"That is the weird part. Oh, Wolf, I had talked myself into not wanting to do the whole dating a celebrity thing. But I've fallen for you. And my heart is jumping up and down because it feels like a win, so...yes, I'll be your girlfriend."

"As my girlfriend, things won't change."

"They won't?" She pouted. "I was hoping that would grant me access to information about the secret apps. Darn! Foiled again. But what about the cameras?"

"Do you think you can handle the unwanted attention? It might get worse. It might not. And I won't argue if you suddenly feel you need to split. But promise me you'll be nice and not ghost me or throw things at me if you do want to break up?"

"Throw things?"

Wolf nodded, then pointed to a scar on his

bicep. "Knife. She was off aim. Just a bit higher and I would have lost an eye."

"Why are people like that? That's just crazy."

"I guess I have a bad eye for picking women." He put up a hand. "Until now. I have a feeling we will work, Ivy. You want to come over after you get off?" he asked.

Did she? Yes and no. She'd already broken her staunch need to keep it at one date by agreeing to be his girlfriend. She needed to get quiet and figure out if she really wanted that or if it had been an exuberant reaction to feeling like a princess who had been claimed by a prince. She needed some space.

"Actually…" She opened the Concierge app on her phone and verified what she'd just remembered. "Ivan and I have a Zoom call with one of the research centers offering an MS study."

"I'll cross my fingers for the both of you."

She kissed him. "See you tomorrow morning." She turned to spy the photogs leaning against a street post. "And so it begins."

CHAPTER ELEVEN

DESPITE BEING TIRED after a long day on her feet, Ivy couldn't begin to touch anything but joy. Since there hadn't been a single camera-wielding paparazzi between Wolf's place and work, she'd dismissed the niggling feeling to end this relationship. How could she end something that had only just begun? If she couldn't withstand a few photographers for someone as wonderful as Wolf then she was seriously missing out on something.

Wolf had picked her up after work, greeted her with a long, delicious kiss, and handed her the calendar page. It read: *Let someone in.*

They'd both shared a knowing glance. Suddenly the calendar had gone all wise and prophetic, seeming to read them both.

Now she stood in his penthouse. It was a total man cave with stone walls and brushed black steel stylings. Massive dark wood furnishings, and a huge TV on the wall. For work, he'd explained. He'd cast his laptop to the screen. In the center of the room hung a four-tiered chandelier of more black iron. It was a two-story, open floorplan, with a black iron staircase hugging one wall. The corner space—the two connecting walls were all windows—looked over an old railyard that the city had rewilded with grass, flowers and trees.

"It's cozy here." She wandered into the kitchen to lean against the black marble countertop. "Feels weirdly homey."

"Why weirdly?" He kissed her and walked around to unpack the food that had been delivered just as they'd arrived. "I like to think I have a little style."

"You do. It's exactly what I'd expect to represent you." That kiss had been too brief. It had ignited something within her that she knew would smolder until answered. "Mm, that smells good."

"You like peanut noodles?"

"Heck, yeah. Hand me a fork. I'm starving."

After much food and wine, and laughter, Wolf said, "I've never met a woman with whom I've been able to really share food. I mean, I can make a pig out of myself and you don't care."

"You go voraciously at what tastes great. You're comfortable around me."

"I am."

"Good, because there's not a thing about me that should be intimidating."

"I think the fact that you're an entomologist is intimidating. You've got bug smarts."

"Ha! Don't even get me started on the order of *coleoptera*. I will talk your head off."

"That's beetles, right? See, I've learned a few things from you already. I've seen pictures of some beetles that look like chrome or a shiny car finish."

"You should see the *polybothrus sumptuosa gema*. It's purple with green flecks on its carapace. Very small. Found in Madagascar. It's one of my favorites."

"Seriously? Show me."

Ivy tugged out her phone and searched for an image. As she did, they moved from the counter to the massive leather couch while she pulled up more images and explained where the beetle could be found and if she'd had opportunity to see it in the wild. She gave him the rock 'n' roll tour of the beetle kingdom.

"The purple and blue ones are my favorites. Wait, I forgot about the *cyclommatus metalifer*. It's got massive pinchers. But even the plain beetles fascinate me. Oh, here I am going off on a wild and boring tour of the beetle kingdom." When she finally glanced out the window to see it was dark, she shoved his shoulder. "I told you not to get me started!"

"What? Everything you've shown me was interesting. But really, there should be an app for beetles. You know, one that identifies them with space for you to add your own images."

"That sounds useful. Make it for me."

"Don't think I won't. I sense bugs are the way to your heart."

"You're a smart man. But there are other ways to my heart." She touched him under the chin, luring him toward her so he scooched closer on the couch. The smolder had only grown heavier, more wanting. "Kiss me."

"Always and whenever you want, Ivy. I like kissing you here..." He leaned in and nuzzled his nose aside her cheek, brushing light kisses on her earlobe. That felt like every fantasy bursting free from the seams and gliding over her skin.

He breathed against her cheek and moved up to feather his lips across her lashes. Ivy twined her fingers into his beard and held him close. Their intimacy felt easy. Not demanding. Yet hungry. She kissed him deeply, wanting to dive into him, discover all that he hid. And yet, she would not touch those places he protected unless he offered her entrance.

"I want to make love to you," he said.

"Well, that's why I'm here, to help you with whatever challenge your calendar presents."

He laughed but silenced quickly. Looking up at her, his hair tousled and his eyes glimmering in the low light, Ivy saw the little boy inside him that still hid behind the barriers.

"This is not about a calendar tonight," he said.

"I know. I was joking." She kissed him and began to unbutton his dress shirt. "This is about us. Finally saying to each other that we trust the other. Do you trust me?"

"Do you trust me?"

"I do. There's nothing about you that comes off as untrustworthy. But I know you've been burned by women, so I expect your trust might not be as easy to win."

Another kiss tasted her lips slowly and ended with a dash of his tongue. "I do trust you. But it still feels like maybe I'm just saying it because that's what you want to hear. Does that make sense?"

"I get it. Don't rush it, Wolf. I'm not going to hurt you. I'm in this for as long as you desire."

"What about the paparazzi? I can feel you tense up whenever they are near."

"Truth? I'm struggling with being a part of your celebrity life. I keep telling myself I don't want it to lead to Ivan and then give him more stress than he's already got, but… I know he's very capable. So maybe it's just an excuse?"

"Could be. Maybe it's best if you just cut and run right now?"

Ivy's jaw dropped open. Was he serious?

Wolf shrugged. "I don't want you to, but I also don't want to do anything to hurt you."

"Thank you. But I don't want to run. Especially not at this part."

"What part is that?"

She bowed her forehead to his and licked the tip of his nose. "The part where we have sex."

"Let's take this upstairs to my bedroom." He stood and held out his hand.

When Ivy stood and took his hand, he suddenly bent and lifted her over his shoulder. She whooped as he carried her up the stairs and dropped her on the bed. The thick, charcoal velvet spread caressed her body.

"See? All that weightlifting is good for something." He unbuttoned his shirt and tugged it off, tossing it aside before giving her a flex of each biceps.

Ivy preened over his incredible physique. Honed hard from his workouts and brushed with more of the soft dark hairs like his beard and moustache. His biceps flexed and his six-pack tempted her onto her knees to touch. He growled as she slid her hand over his abdomen and around to clutch his derriere.

A kiss to his chest devoured his essence. He smelled like peanut sauce and wine. Desire had reached full capacity. She had to answer it. Now.

With a tug, he pulled the cloth-wrapped tie from her ponytail and then glided his fingers through her hair.

He kneeled on the bed. Face to face, they explored one another. His hands gliding under her T-shirt and pulling it off to toss. Wolf laughed when he saw her bra. "I should have guessed!"

So she had the one bra with butterflies on it. She wasn't about to apologize for being the crazy bug lady.

When he bowed to kiss her breasts and tugged down the bra cup to tongue her nipple, Ivy clawed her nails gently but firmly down his back. "That's so good."

"You got a little wild to you?" He growled and gave her a gentle bite, which only rocketed up the giddy want swirling in her core. With another tug, he pushed down her jeans and panties and tossed them aside. He stood to remove his pants, and when he stood naked before her, Ivy leaned back on her hands and admired his physique.

"What?" He shrugged.

"I certainly hope you're not going to be shy with that."

He leaned over her, kissing down her neck and to her breasts. "You got it."

Wolf stared up at the black spot on the ceiling and frowned. It moved. A spider? Better that than a cockroach, of which he'd seen far too many times since moving to the States. He should be thankful it wasn't larger.

Beside him lay a long stretch of soft warmth. Ivy's hair spilled across his arm and shoulder. The sage scent from the potpourri thingy he'd bought on a whim mingled with her heat and skin, filling his nostrils with a heady remembrance of last night. That had been some sex. Intimate and feisty. Fiery and fast. They'd both gone at each other as if they'd known exactly what the other desired. So cool, especially since first-time sex with women usually resulted in some awkwardness, much faster climax than usual, and sometimes even the woman getting all demanding and weird or even submissive.

Wolf had never been with a woman who had known exactly what she wanted. At the same time, he'd felt an equal partner in their give-and-take. Ivy Quinn was one hell of a woman. Who knew how to pour a wicked cup of coffee.

He had to smile to think that he'd found her

in the shop in his building, and it had taken him weeks before he'd rustled up the courage to talk to her. And now that he had? This beautiful woman wanted to be in his life. And without asking for his money. It didn't feel possible.

Well. She'd been right about guessing his trust wasn't completely there yet. Something could still happen that would send him reeling. It always happened. So he would be cautious. He didn't know any other way to walk through life. Keep to himself, protect his boundaries, and always be the first to walk away. Those precautions kept Wolfgang Zeigler's heart protected.

The flash drive the PI had sent him still sat in his desk drawer. A smart man would make sure he knew what he was getting into. But Ivy trusted him. And if he opened that envelope then he shattered that earned trust. Besides, she was still leery about the photogs. He had to make this as easy for her as possible.

When she stirred beside him, he turned his head to nuzzle into her hair. The princess between his sheets lifted her head. She blew at the hair tangled over her face.

"Morning," he offered.

"Sure."

Not a morning person? Maybe she needed coffee.

When her hand slid across his stomach and moved lower, all thoughts of coffee vanished.

"You think so?" he teased.

"I do."

Wolf snickered. "Good call. But can we move it off the bed? Maybe into the shower?"

"But I'm so comfy and warm right here against your big, hard—" she gave him a squeeze "—mmm."

"I'm just a little freaked that spider up there will drop on us when we're going at it."

Ivy rolled to her back and squinted to pinpoint the black spot he'd kept in his sight since opening his eyes. *"Pholcidae,"* she said on a yawn. "Just a daddy longlegs. It won't bite."

"I did not need to hear that." He sat up and pushed the covers off Ivy to reveal her curling up into a reactive ball. "Come on!"

CHAPTER TWELVE

APPARENTLY THE MAN was a morning person. Something Ivy could never relate to, but knew she had to incorporate into her life if she ever wanted to hold a decent-paying job. On the other hand, field research tended to follow the project leader's timeline, and that was her ultimate goal. Stalking through the Amazon in search of the blushing phantom butterfly? Let's get together after noon, team, because that particular insect doesn't come out until dusk.

But Wolf had gotten out of bed, muttering about the spider. And his bare derriere had lured her to follow him into the shower. The quick burst of cold water had made her yelp. She'd forgotten that was one of his kinks. He'd quickly comforted her shivers by turning her to face the wall and kissing down her shoulder. They fit perfectly. And thank that spider for the shower sex, right?

Now they stood before the marble vanity,

morning sunlight beaming through a high, long window. The mirror reflected his clever grin as he cupped her breasts and thrust inside her from behind. The sight of his big hand covering her breast amped up the erotic thrill. That slightly sneaky smile—his sex smile—was something she would never get from her thoughts.

When he came, he hugged her tightly against his body and his shudders vibrated her very bones. But he wasn't greedy. Slipping his hand around and down between her legs, he masterfully brought her to a shivering climax.

"Do you have to work today?" he whispered.

"Nope."

"Then we're doing this all day. I'm going to order in some breakfast. You like eggs or pancakes?"

"Both."

He nuzzled a hard kiss against her neck, and she reached back to run her fingers up through his thick hair.

"Stay naked," he murmured, then stepped back, winked at her in the mirror, and left.

Ivy nodded at her reflection. That handsome, bearded wolf of a man was all hers? What a ride. This makeshift princess really had found a prince charming. A reluctant billionaire who sought a simple life amid the chaos of his reality. And she had been able to step beyond her cautious worries to embrace it all.

Out in the bedroom, she navigated around the tousled bed sheets that lay on the floor and a pillow that lay against the wall. She smiled to recall their lusty antics. She glanced overhead but did not spy the arachnid.

She plopped onto the bed and scanned the floor, spying her phone peeking out from under her discarded shirt. She picked it up and saw a missed call from ten minutes earlier. When she'd been in the shower? She clicked through. It was...

"Heather?"

Suddenly, the freedom she had been luxuriating in swooshed out through her pores. Her body tensed.

She called the number and Heather answered immediately. "Ivy, I'm so glad you called back. It's Ivan."

"What is it?" Her heartbeats thundered to top speed. Ivy clutched a sheet against her chest.

"He was unresponsive when I checked in on him this morning. His breathing was—I had to call the ambulance. We're at the ER. Can you get here?"

"Of course. I'm on my way right now. Is he...?"

"They were able to revive him. I haven't spoken to the doctor. Just get here, okay?"

"Yes." Ivy hung up and dove for her clothes.

"Eggs, pancakes, and—" Wolf stopped in the bedroom doorway.

He was naked and Ivy didn't take a moment to even look at him.

"What's up?"

"It's Ivan. His physical therapist tried to call ten minutes ago. He's in the ER."

Wolf swore. "You're heading there?"

"Of course. I can't believe I did this!"

"Did what? Ivy, don't blame yourself—"

"Don't tell me what to think!" she snapped. She pulled her T-shirt over her head then grabbed her shoes.

"I won't. I'm sorry. I'll call a ride for you."

"No, I can—" She stopped in the doorway. She didn't have a vehicle. And the hospital was a subway ride away. While panic set her nerves to a buzz and made her shake, she had the sense to realize her best, and quickest, route to the hospital. "Yes. I'll take that offer for a ride."

"Let me get some clothes on," he said and disappeared into the walk-in closet. Less than a minute later he appeared, zipping up his jeans and pulling on a T-shirt. "Let's go."

Ivan had taken the wrong medication, which had resulted in an overdose. The pill bottles were the same size and color and the pill shapes had been remarkably close, so it had been, unfortunately, an easy mishap. And with his vision blurry in the one eye, he may have made the mistake no matter what.

He was stable now, and the doctor told Ivy that a night in the hospital, some fluids, and careful monitoring would see him home in better shape. It hadn't been something she or Heather could have anticipated. It was just a mistake. He also suggested Heather label Ivan's pill bottles with a larger font.

Ivy thanked him then went to sit at Ivan's bedside. He was sleeping, so she let him rest. There was no place she wanted to be right now. Estelle had told her it was no problem to miss a day or two at But First... Coffee was not as important as family.

Wolf had accompanied her here and had stepped aside when the doctor had wanted to speak specifically to Ivy. She briefly wondered if he had left, then her brain wouldn't allow her to do anything more than focus on Ivan.

She clasped her shaking hands together on her lap. She had been out of the house, enjoying herself with Wolf. It was difficult to even consider how she had been so lacking in concern for her brother's safety. She was not prepared to experience the loss of a family member again.

Damn it, why had she thought she had the

right to something so self-indulgent as sex? Last night had been good. Seeing fireworks explode, good. But now she was being punished for her selfishness. There was just no getting beyond that truth.

Late in the afternoon, Ivan woke. He was groggy but managed a smile. He apologized to her, and that made Ivy feel even worse. None of this was his fault. He hadn't asked for this disease. And he'd been nothing but positive since learning about it. She didn't tell him she'd been having sex with Wolf. Her brother wasn't stupid. He knew where she had been.

"You should go rest," Ivan said quietly. "You look tired."

"I'm fine." Hungry, but she'd manage. "I'm not going to leave your side."

"You can't be by my side forever, Ivy. Things will happen. It's something we have to accept."

"We don't have to accept anything, Ivan. We'll figure this life out for you. This will get better. It has to," she said on a failing tone.

All she wanted to do was cry. To bury her head against someone's shoulder and bawl. She'd failed Ivan. And she'd almost lost him. What she wouldn't give to have her parents here right now to support and hug her.

"At the very least, will you move to the sofa by the window?" Ivan asked. "You're making me nervous sitting so close. Your jaw pulses when you're tense. Just stretch out for a while. Take a nap. It'll make me feel better."

She eyed the sofa. Short, flat, not designed for comfort. Yet, it did appeal. "Maybe just ten minutes. You rest, too. The doctor comes back on shift later this evening, and I want to talk to him and see if he has any info about local studies."

"You're a trooper, sis."

She got up and her bones protested after having sat on the hard chair for half the day with only one bathroom break. Feeling older than her years, Ivy crept over to the sofa and lay down, her head landing on the armrest, and her legs bending to tuck her feet against the other end. Ivan winked at her. He was getting back some of his energy. That made her feel a minuscule better.

And with that small hope to assuage her fears, she closed her eyes.

Wolf had been at the hospital since bringing Ivy here this morning. He'd peeked in a few times but each time her body language had told him to stay away. By mid-afternoon his stomach had begun to growl. And if his was growling, he knew Ivy's would be also. He slipped out to pick up some food.

He hated that he couldn't sit beside her and

hold her hand. Offer his shoulder for her head to rest on. But he didn't want to overstep her boundaries. He was familiar with personal boundaries. And even though they'd exploded those barriers last night, he suspected she might be feeling some guilt over their antics. She'd been away the one night her brother had needed someone to help him. It had been a random incident. But Wolf also felt extreme guilt.

And there wasn't any way to make it better. He couldn't throw money at the problem because what was done was done. Ivan was now recovering. But he had heard the conversation suggesting the medications could be labeled with larger fonts and color coding. And that had sparked an idea. He'd tugged out his phone and researched, finding some pharmacies did color code their bottles, but they still used the same amber-colored plastic or white containers. He made a note to investigate pharmaceutical innovations.

Now, with food in hand, he looked inside the room. Ivan sat upright in the hospital bed, a woman leaning over him and—

Ivan tilted his head to eye Wolf. The woman, with long pink dreads and a cupid bow smile, stepped back and smoothed down her scrubs. A nurse? Not if they'd been doing what Wolf had just caught them doing.

With a glance around the room, Wolf saw Ivy sleeping on the sofa.

He stepped inside and whispered, "Hey, man, I'm Wolf Zeigler. Uh, your sister's…boyfriend?"

"You don't sound very sure of that," Ivan replied in a quiet voice. They both glanced to Ivy. Still asleep.

Wolf walked inside and stopped at Ivan's bedside. "We just made the labels official."

The woman kissed Ivan on the forehead and told him she'd leave him for a bit. "I'm Heather," she said to Wolf. "Ivan's physical therapist."

"I've heard about you. Nice to meet you."

"I'll leave you two alone." She left quickly.

Wolf held up the bag. "I brought food for Ivy. She's been holding vigil."

"She feels guilty. I wish she wouldn't."

"Hard not to. I feel the same having been the one who kept your sister from your side. How are you feeling?"

"Better. It was a quirk what happened. It wasn't Ivy's fault. And even if she had been home, asleep in her room, it still would have happened and she wouldn't have found me until she woke. Don't let it bother you. What food did you bring?"

"Sandwiches. You hungry?"

"I'm starving. And if Ivy's going to sleep then I'm taking half her sandwich."

Wolf sat and quietly pulled out the sandwiches so as not to wake the sleeping beauty. He offered Ivan the ham on rye and he halved it then handed Wolf back the rest to save for Ivy.

"So," Wolf said around a bite of pastrami. "How long have you and Heather been a thing?"

Ivan paused with the sandwich before his mouth.

Wolf couldn't prevent a grin. "Just calling it like I see it."

"Don't tell her," Ivan said with a nod toward the couch. "We haven't figured out how to do that yet. Ivy might not like the hired help getting involved with her brother."

"I don't know. She's pretty easygoing."

"Yeah, but we are paying Heather. So… Just keep it quiet for now."

"Not a problem."

"So you finally decided to make my sister an official girlfriend? Page Six and everything?"

"She seems to like hanging out with me despite the circus that follows. Uh, I hope it didn't upset you?"

Ivan shrugged. "I just want my sister to be safe. It's gotta suck, having to dodge the press."

"My entire dating history sucks, man. I'm pretty cautious around women."

"I read the reference to your past paramours. My sister is not a gold digger."

"I know that. She's good stuff. Ivy is…" Wolf blew out a breath. Brothers didn't know everything about their sisters. That file in his desk drawer haunted him. Should he read it? "Do I even deserve someone so special as her?"

"Time will tell. And a discerning brother." Ivan set the sandwich on his lap. "So I've always wanted to ask a man who has billions what he spends his money on?"

"Cutting right to the chase, eh?"

"If it's not too personal. What kind of car do you have? What's the most extravagant purchase you've made? Give me something here. I need a little fantasy to brighten my day."

"I don't drive," he offered to Ivan. "I know how to, but New York traffic makes a sane man crazy."

"I hear you. I'm a bike man myself."

"Ivy told me you planned to bike across the United States?"

"Yeah, that was a dream. Not sure I'll ever be able to sit on a bike again. It's my balance." Ivan swore.

Wolf could feel his pain. And in that moment, he knew he'd never been so devastated by life as this man had been. He may have struggled as a child, fending for himself in foster care and learning to survive, but life had not stolen his freedom.

"How about one of those fixed-position indoor bikes? A fancy one with the screen you can watch so it looks like you're biking outdoors?"

Ivan shrugged. "Let's not talk about my inability to be normal. You didn't tell me your craziest purchase."

"I haven't made any crazy purchases." Well, beyond the diamond ring that had brought on the lawsuit. "Too much money can be too much of a good thing."

"I can't believe that. There's got to be something you've always wanted?"

Indeed, but that was an intangible a man could never buy. Love and the constancy of family did not come with a price tag. Was Ivy the sort who could ever be happy living in a little village with toddlers chasing through the garden?

No, she needed to study the insects in that garden. Kids might get in her way. He shouldn't imagine too much about what she wanted from life. Nor should he expect he deserved such a woman as her.

"I do like motorcycles," he offered as a means to entertain Ivan's request. "Maybe someday, when I move home to Germany, I'll get a Ducati and cruise the Autobahn."

"Sounds wonderful. The wind blowing through your hair. Your body capable of responding to what you ask of it."

Wolf slapped a hand on Ivan's shoulder. "Just know, man, that I'm here for you. I care about your sister and want to see her happy. And that means you're coming along for that ride."

"Sounds like a bumpy one, but those are the best kind. But you better treat her well. Because if you don't…"

"I'll have to answer to you."

Ivy stirred on the sofa. Ivan shoved his half-eaten sandwich toward Wolf, who immediately figured that Ivy might be upset to see her brother noshing on non-hospital-approved food, and he gobbled it up as he walked over to the sofa. "Hey there, sleepyhead."

"Wolf. You're…still here?"

"I brought some food. You've been going all day. I knew you'd be hungry."

"Bless you."

"Got to meet your brother as well," he added with a wink toward Ivan that Ivy could not see. That sandwich sat at the base of his throat, he'd gobbled it so fast. "You two are cut from the same cloth, that's for sure."

"Stubborn, independent and assertive?" Ivan said.

"Exactly." Wolf chuckled and then grabbed the sandwich bag for Ivy.

She bypassed his offer and went to the bedside and took her brother's hand. "How are you feeling?"

"Whipped, but I'll survive. You eat something. Then you can go home with your boyfriend."

"My—" She glanced over her shoulder. "You two did have a talk, eh?"

Wolf shrugged. "Was that supposed to be a secret?"

"No." She sat beside the bed and Wolf set the food bag on the tray beside her. "I'm not going home until the doctor says you're out of the woods and signs you out."

"Ivy, I'm good now."

"Yes, but—Ivan, don't argue, please?"

"Fine. Stay. But I'm not great company."

"I've known that for twenty-some years." She opened the bag and took out a sandwich. "You should go," she said to Wolf. "I appreciate you hanging around all day. But like Ivan said, he's good. We can take it from here."

An abrupt dismissal. Wolf almost took offense. But this was a family matter. He didn't want to intrude.

"Will you give me a call before you turn in for the night?" he asked as he leaned close to her, sliding a hand across her back. He felt her melt against his palm, responding with a sigh.

"I'll make sure she does," Ivan said. "Thanks, man."

"Not a problem." Wolf kissed Ivy on the cheek. Too quick. He hated walking away. Leaving that beautiful woman behind.

In the hallway, he passed Heather, who was headed back toward Ivan's room. Weird that Ivan didn't want Ivy to know. Then again, she may be upset that her brother was—well, why couldn't he have a relationship, hell, a healthy sex life, if it was there for him?

And as for offering to help them financially, what could be so terrible about that? Ivy's defensive stance against any monetary help was like…well, it was how he acted when he wanted to control a situation. Wolf pushed everyone away.

But since meeting Ivy, all he'd been doing was pulling her closer. She had changed him. And he wouldn't argue that change. But in the process, had she become more protective of her heart?

CHAPTER THIRTEEN

IVY AGREED TO leave the hospital after the doctor told her Ivan was doing well and could be released in the morning. She was exhausted and hadn't slept much beyond the nap on the couch. Now she texted Wolf a quick "See you in a few days. Ivan coming home tomorrow. I'm staying with him for a day." Then she hit the sack and was asleep within minutes.

The next day, after Ivan arrived home, she watched him like a hawk. Heather had relabeled his medication bottles, but Ivy had insisted she had things under control and told her to leave. She spent the day filling out more study applications and helping Ivan browse for online jobs. He needed something that would appeal to his adventurous and active heart, but without requiring him to leave the home. Or located at a facility that catered to his physical needs. It was a tall order, but not impossible.

Browsing an online retail site, she eyed the

stationary bike with the electronic screen that was supposed to immerse the user in a virtual experience of biking through meadows or across the country or even in Paris. It was costly, but no more expensive than some of his medical bills. But where to put it if Ivan was out of this place early next year? He couldn't travel with it. She put it on her wish list, for a future that might see her brother in a permanent home.

Ivan was the one to let out a hoot when he found a coaching job that offered virtual training for athletes. The home office was in London, but their employees were stationed all over the world. He filled out an application, then Ivy made him something to eat.

They could do this. She just needed...

One of those big bear hugs from Wolf. Because that was capable of changing her world.

"No coffee today, boss?"

Wolf didn't look up when Stacy entered his office. She set a stack of mail on his desk. He'd foregone stopping for coffee this morning, knowing his favorite barista wouldn't be there to serve him. He planned to stop at Ivan's brownstone after work.

"Busy," he muttered, without looking up from the computer screen.

"You want to do a bar hop with a bunch of us later?"

The invitation took him by surprise. No one in the office had ever invited him to any sort of extracurricular activity outside of work. Not in the three years Concierge had been in this building. He'd heard the gossip; he was a liability with the paparazzi hanging on his every move.

He narrowed his brows at Stacy.

She shrugged. "Figured you might like to join us. It's always couples. And since you and Ivy are a thing, and she's not so—well, you'll fit in now. She was nice, by the way. You surprised us all that night. Thought for sure you'd sworn off women."

"Never say never, Stacy. I'll pass on the bar hop." Much as he wouldn't mind getting to know his employees in a more casual setting. "Ivy's brother isn't well. She's taking care of him and—we're busy."

"Oh, sorry. Is he going to be okay?"

"It's a complicated situation. But thanks for the offer. Maybe next time?"

"Sure. We just got confirmation from Dyna-Tech on the contract. I'll send the closing documents to you for a signature."

"Excellent. I'm hoping to meet in person with the CEO very soon."

That company was helping Concierge to expand to more services and insert themselves in the major socials and search engines. It was a natural alignment that made a lot of sense and would see the Concierge name everywhere, from cell phones to televisions to even household appliances. The sky was the limit.

Yet, as exciting as that future for his company was, Wolf found that with every step he moved Concierge forward, he wanted to take a step away. Completely offload the company and go off on his own? Not quite so extreme. He liked to guide the path. It was his product. He felt as though his name and reputation were on every single tap of the app and product that may eventually carry the name.

But he could do it from a different country. That little cottage in the German countryside. A wife. Kids. More and more he could imagine settling into that cottage with Ivy. Of course, she wasn't the settling type. She had a career waiting for her to explore. And he loved that.

Ivy was not so...

Not so what? Stacy hadn't finished that statement, but Wolf suspected it would have ended with something like "surface," "materialistic," or even "greedy," as would aptly label his previous girlfriends.

He opened the drawer and eyed the flash drive. The private investigator always delivered the reports on a flash drive so nothing could be traced via email. The previous time he'd gotten a report, it had detailed the woman's criminal record. He'd dodged a bullet with that one. Ivy's report could be completely blank. She had no skeletons in her closet. He knew that.

So he closed the drawer and left the office for the day.

While walking toward Ivy's neighborhood, Wolf swung inside a flower shop to pick up a dozen—Ivy didn't seem like the classic roses kind of girl. He perused the assorted bouquets and decided on a frilly purple flower the clerk called beebalm. Perfect. It had the name of a bug in it!

The jewelry boutique next to the flower shop featured an elaborate diamond necklace in the window. He paused but then shook his head. Not Ivy's style. And he could imagine her outrage should he spend so much money on her. She was the opposite of any woman he had dated in the past few years. And while he should be rejoicing that fact, it hurt his heart in a way that surprised him. By not accepting his money, it felt as though she was rejecting him.

What was wrong with him that he needed to use money as a means to validation? Maybe she should be the one ordering a background check on him instead of the other way around.

Ivy Quinn was a normal woman with a normal life and some challenges. He, on the other hand, was not fit to walk alongside her. How could she see beyond his hang-ups and rules about money and dating?

He stared into the flower bouquet. Should he stick to models and money-hungry actresses? Maybe that was his lane? It was certainly the slot the world tried to jam him into.

He shook his head. Square Wolf did not fit in those circular slots. And Ivy didn't even have a shape. She was free and open. She'd already smoothed some of his sharp corners. He couldn't mess up. Losing her didn't seem feasible.

At the brownstone, Ivan greeted him at the door, standing quite steadily with the aid of a cane.

"Wolf, come in. Ivy is making cookies and her hands are covered in dough." He closed the door, then carefully turned and made a slow beeline to the sofa, where he sat.

Wolf wandered into the kitchen where he found his girlfriend elbow deep in cookie dough. It smelled like chocolate and sugar. Something white smudged her cheek. He kissed her there. "Ugh. That wasn't sugar."

"Probably flour," she said. "Have a seat. Did you bring flowers for Ivan?"

"If he likes beebalm, I guess so."

"I'm allergic," Ivan called from the living room. "Let Ivy have them."

"Well, there you go." Wolf presented the bouquet to her. "Second choice, but it'll have to do."

She bent to sniff the bouquet, dough-covered hands held near her shoulders. "Mm, I love that oregano scent."

"Oregano?" Wolf sniffed the bouquet and it did have a strange pizza scent to it. "Weird."

"You can use the leaves for some traditional remedies. Not sure what, exactly. Thank you." She kissed him. "I'll keep them in my room so they won't bother Ivan. Will you put them in something for me? There might be a vase under the sink."

Wolf found the vase while Ivy pulled a pan of steaming cookies from the oven and replaced it with another that held globs of raw dough.

"We both had a craving," she offered. "Will you commandeer that spatula and put a couple on a plate for Ivan?"

Happy to help, Wolf shoveled three huge cookies onto a plate then handed it off to her brother. He'd never known a foster mom who would bake for him. Most meals had been from a box, fast food, or leftovers.

That's the past, man. You're here. Right now. Make this a moment.

Wolf claimed a cookie for himself. "I don't

think I've ever had a fresh-baked chocolate chip cookie before."

"Seriously? You must have had a poor childhood—oh." Ivy's shoulders dropped. "Sorry. You eat as many as you like. After I pull this last batch from the oven, we'll go sit in the park and devour them. How does that sound?"

"Like my best day ever."

Ivy finished her second cookie. Wolf had eaten half a dozen. She was glad because the recipe had made four dozen. Far too many for just she and Ivan.

"My domesticity is showing," she said as a biker cruised before them on the sidewalk.

"I'm thankful for it. Like I said, I've never had a fresh-baked homemade cookie. I would pay serious cash for more of this."

"Save your money. I'll make them more often and make sure you get a dozen every time I do."

He leaned in and kissed her. She tasted like chocolate. "Your brother looks like he's doing well?"

"Well as he can be. His vision is less blurry today. In some cases, the eye problem goes away after a few months. I just hope it doesn't become…" She looked away from him, unable to speak the worst thing she could imagine.

"Don't think ahead like that," Wolf said. "Take

it day by day. And he's got Heather stopping in, too. That must help a lot."

"She's got to stop coming by when she's not scheduled. We can't pay for those extra hours."

Wolf took her hand and squeezed it against his chest. "I wouldn't worry about Heather and Ivan. In fact, I suspect she wouldn't mind a little extra time with your brother. Maybe a weekend alone?"

"What are you implying? She has a full-time job that keeps her busy."

He shrugged. "Have you paid attention to those two together?"

"Well, I—" Ivy gaped at him. "Are you suggesting…?"

Wolf raised a brow and shrugged.

"Ivan would tell me if they were—they can't be. What makes you think so?"

"Just a suspicion. But back to the weekend off idea. I have a proposal for you."

"Oh, yeah?"

"I have to fly to Venice this Friday. I've got a meeting with the company that is going to take Concierge to the next level. I plan to stay the weekend in my palazzo. So… I'm wondering if you would like to come along to Venice with me? I'd only leave you on your own for an afternoon while I take care of business, then I promise the rest of the time would be for touristy stuff and lots of sex."

That last part sounded wonderful. And so did the part about flying to Venice. But really, did the man not pick up on her angst? She'd just barely avoided losing her brother because she hadn't been home to help him with his medication, and now he wanted to whisk her away for an entire weekend?

"I can't leave Ivan that long. He needs to be my priority."

"Heather can stay with him. And like I said, they might enjoy the time together. Alone."

"I still don't get why you think they are having a thing. Unless Ivan said something to you?"

"Just a guess."

"Well, even if that was so, I can't afford to hire Heather for an entire weekend."

"I'll hire her. And I won't take a no from you. This is something I want, Ivy, and I'm willing to put my money where my mouth is."

"Don't you understand what I'm going through? Wolf, it's as if you don't know me at all."

"Is it what *you* are going through," he challenged, "or rather, what your brother is going through?"

"I don't—" She closed her mouth.

He had a point. And she hated that he did have a point. Because it put her in the wrong. She didn't have the emotional head space to devote to both caring for Ivan and keeping a romance with Wolf going. For one night she'd felt she could manage it, and look what had happened! Regret overwhelmed her desire for romance. She couldn't possibly enjoy herself while Ivan was home alone suffering.

"I can't do this." She stood, and when Wolf took her hand she shook it away. "I don't want your money. I never want your money. You can't buy my cooperation. Or my love! This is my problem to handle. Good night. I'll... You can text me later."

She hurried across the street and disappeared inside the brownstone.

Wolf pushed his hands over his face and leaned forward, catching his elbows on his knees. Ivy's statement about him trying to buy her cooperation—her love—knocked the wind out of him. It immediately shot him back to when he was a kid, trying to survive in the foster system. He'd been scrawny, quiet, and an easy target for the older siblings who he would never call actual brothers. They had kicked him, called him names, taken his food, and pissed on his sheets. Until finally he'd gotten smart and started using his meager paper route money to buy them off. That had quickly turned into a shakedown on their part. But as long as he handed over his money, he hadn't gotten a black eye and had clean sheets.

He was ashamed that he'd had to go to such lengths. And angry that his foster parents had not made it stop. It had been a vicious cycle. Never had he felt wanted. Easily disposed of at the whim of a family who would never love or really care for him.

Ivy had just walked away from him, leaving him alone. Overlooked. Disposed.

He swore and shook his head. Ivy couldn't know the minute details of his history. How such desperation had pushed him to offer others money to ensure his own safety. To buy a little kindness. The facsimile of love. But he hadn't offered her money to make something in his life better.

Or had he? Was he trying to keep Ivy by the same means he had utilized when younger? Was he truly buying her love?

"No." He shook his head. "Why does money always seem to jam a wedge in any relationship I have?"

It was different this time, though. Ivy wasn't insisting he pay for her dinners or clothes or even trips. She couldn't care less about his money. It was him trying to get something from another person. Something like…

He had seen the caring, loving relationship the Quinn siblings shared. *Love.* All he wanted was to feel loved. He had begun to relax and loosen his shoulders and believe that maybe it could happen with Ivy. She made his days brighter. She enjoyed spending time with him. He thought of her every moment that numbers and code did not fill his brain. She was everything he had never thought he needed.

He turned a look over his shoulder at the brownstone. He couldn't screw this up. He didn't want to lose the best thing that had ever walked into his life.

But had that just happened?

CHAPTER FOURTEEN

IVY BREWED COFFEE and scrambled eggs. Ivan had just woken and called for her to help him shave. She did not mind helping her brother do the things he was losing control over. It made her sad, though, to see him want to hold the razor, knowing he was too shaky to do so. She'd reassured him that it was early. He was usually much steadier in the afternoons.

He'd said he could dress himself, so she left him to it, but would be there to help if he called.

With a sigh, her thoughts switched to how she'd walked away from Wolf last night. That had been wrong. She didn't want to alienate him from her life by treating him as if he weren't worthy of being a part of that life. All things included. But the offer to help Ivan had, once again, put up her backbone. And yet, she knew Wolf had only offered out of kindness.

Did she really believe she couldn't juggle Ivan's care and a romance with Wolf? Some moments she did. But after sleeping on it, she realized that was an excuse to not step up and embrace the good that life was offering her.

She slid the eggs onto a plate and covered it with another plate to keep it warm, then plucked the toast from the toaster and buttered it.

Would their lives be different now if they had taken the settlement money from the boat manufacturer? What had they really gained by standing firm and refusing to be silenced? They had spoken out regarding the faulty parts on only one television interview. The company had issued a recall on the part. End of story.

That money would have been helpful now. But still. No. She shook her head. She felt good with that decision. Morally.

"You can't buy my love."

She never should have said that to Wolf. It had slipped out. She hadn't meant it. Had she?

"No." But she may have screwed up the opportunity life had given her for good.

Ivan walked into the kitchen with the use of his cane, a curve of aluminum emblazoned with red and purple flames. He had a big smile on his face. "I love scrambled eggs and toast. Thanks, sis."

"Ivan…" He sat down at the table and she set his plate and coffee before him. "Do you still feel like we made the right choice regarding the settlement money?"

"One hundred percent." He dove into the eggs with a fork. Only after many bites did he stop to meet her gaze. "Why? Are you having second thoughts?"

"That money would come in handy now."

"It would. But we didn't know that at the time. And had we known I was going to fall apart like this, would we still have made the same decision? I hope so."

"You're quite morally straight. Just like mom. Always walking the right path."

"You think I don't make mistakes?"

"Name one." She sat across the table with him and bit into the crunchy toast.

"How about that time I biked through White Mountain National Forest and should have taken a compass?"

"You survived two days and finally found your way out. You were prepared. You didn't starve or lack water. I like to believe it was meant to happen that way. Aren't you the one who is always saying there are no coincidences in life?"

"Exactly. We make the moves and decisions that are meant to be made. Not taking that money? Meant to be."

"I'm not quite so fate-based as you are."

"I'm going to make it through this, Ivy." He clasped her hand. "Promise."

"I know you will."

"Then what's with your sad face? Is it Wolf? I like the guy. He seems to be head over heels for you."

"You think so?" Then why had she walked away from him again last night? "Ivan, he…he offered to pay for your medical bills. I refused. But then, this morning I'm thinking, is it even my place to say yay or nay? It's your health. The money would help you. You should have some say in the matter."

"He didn't make the offer to me. It's your call, sis."

Ivy exhaled dramatically and set her fork down with a clang. "I don't want it to be my call. And he probably didn't make the offer to you because I've been so firm in refusing him. Tell me what you would say if he made that offer to you?"

Ivan shrugged, teased at his remaining eggs with a fork. "I don't know. I've only met the guy a couple times. But I do suspect he's really thrown for you. He is a great guy, Ivy."

"That's not the question I want you to answer."

He set down his fork and wobbled his head, something he did when he was thinking. "Maybe?"

Her heart dropped. "I knew I shouldn't have

refused him. And now I can hardly go back and ask for his help. It would make me like all those other women who hurt him in previous relationships."

"Ivy." Ivan leaned in and put an elbow on the table. "Don't stress about this. I want you to enjoy what you have with Wolf. I know me and Heather are…"

"You and Heather?" Wolf had suggested there might be something going on between the two of them. "Really?"

Ivan shrugged. "I think I've fallen in love. And she feels the same."

"Wow. That was fast." But no quicker than she had fallen for Wolf. When the right people came together, things did seem to click. "I'm happy for you, Ivan. Though I wish you wouldn't have felt you had to hide it from me."

"Heather didn't think it wise. Employer-employee kind of thing, you know."

"Maybe she'll give you a discount on the home visits?" she joked.

He laughed. "I wouldn't dream of asking her such a thing."

"I know. She's worth every penny. I believe she's been a huge part in you retaining your confidence and positivity. And if she's someone you enjoy spending time with, then that makes me happy." She patted his hand. "I have to get dressed and go to work."

"I'll clean up the dishes."

"Oh, I can do——"

"Absolutely not." He grabbed her plate from her. "Let me do what I'm still able to do. It gives me some sense of accomplishment. Okay?"

With a nod, she relented. Who was she to steal any bits of independence he might still retain?

Back in her room, Ivy tugged on a T-shirt and green chinos then stood before the mirror and pulled her hair back into a neat ponytail. The woman in the mirror smiled at the news her brother had found someone he loved. And then the smile dropped. Did that mean she was no longer needed in Ivan's life? Heather could certainly care for him and make him happy.

While the prospect of returning to the life she had put on hold should make her jump for joy, it felt as if the lack of need for her presence in her brother's life hurt. Being needed had been the one thing to keep her going.

As well, it was the only argument that kept her from completely diving into the relationship with Wolf. Was that it? Was she afraid to grab that happiness? It wasn't that she didn't deserve it, it was that she couldn't enjoy it if Ivan wasn't also happy.

The thought was selfish. Ivy hated that she could think like that.

But now she wondered if Wolf had felt much the same when she'd told him she didn't need his help?

On Wednesday, Wolf's calendar read: *Invent a new business.*

So he leaned back in his office chair, closed his eyes, and thought about it. Eventually the craziest ideas spun in his gray matter.

Midnight cookie delivery—hot and with ice cream on the side.

Doggie Dating.

Rent-a-Scholar.

LawnDashers—just click on the app to arrange a lawn mowing.

It was enjoyable, and a practice in allowing his brain to shift from left to right for some creativity. But ultimately, he veered back toward his medical labeling idea. He'd made some contacts. They'd been as excited about the idea as he was.

Since Ivy had come into his life, she had inspired him to seek new ways to give away his money and he had begun to feel as if the money weight was lifting from his shoulders. It was time to stop grumbling about the bad things money brought to his life and instead of reacting, be more active. And besides new business ideas, charitable contributions were a must.

Now that, he could do.

He glanced at the clock. Ten a.m. He had to finish coding this current assignment before noon. He wasn't sure what Ivy thought of him after she'd left him alone on the park bench yesterday. He'd send someone down to collect coffee and a slice of cake.

On Thursday, Ivy wondered what Wolf's calendar asked of him. And what it had asked yesterday. He hadn't come in for coffee. She'd texted him last night before going to bed.

Miss you. See you tomorrow?

He hadn't texted back.

This was bad. He must hate her for her refusal. For treating him like his money was no good. She hadn't meant for it to come out like that, but she completely understood how he must view it. She should apologize.

"Ivy!"

Estelle's shout zapped her back to the present. Ivy saw the espresso machine overflowing and jumped. Coffee spattered her apron. The customer shook his head. And Estelle took over.

"Your head is not in the game today, sweetie."

Estelle wiped the cup and handed it to the customer. "On the house, sir." Then to Ivy she asked, "What's up? It's Mr. Sexy, isn't it?"

"Mr. Sexy? When did we give him that name?"

"Oh, I've always called him that. In my dreams. Don't worry, I don't dream about him—too much—since you two became a couple. Okay, maybe every other day."

"Dream about him all you like." She wanted to say *because he's mine*, but she wasn't sure anymore if he was. "We're just having a tiff. That's why my brain is not focusing."

"A tiff? You know your tiff cost us a coffee and cake yesterday. And I'm not so sure he'll be in this morning either."

"You're really going to lay the loss of ten dollars on my head because of a romantic setback?"

"Oh, it's a setback now? See, that's more than a tiff."

"We just… It's hard for me to parse the two of us being together. I mean, he's so rich."

"Money has nothing to do with love, sweetie."

"I know that. My brother knows that. Why am I finding it so difficult to just let Wolf be Wolf?"

"Yeah, why are you?" came a deep male voice from behind her and across the counter.

Ivy gave Estelle an admonishing face—she could have told her Wolf had walked in—and then turned to smile at him. "Good morning. Coffee and cake?"

"Always. So you don't want me to be me?"

She poured coffee while Estelle grabbed a slice of chocolate chip cake and set it on the counter before him before slipping into the back room.

"I do want you to be you." She set the coffee cup before him. "I'm sorry," she said quietly, casting a glance around the coffee shop. About half a dozen patrons, each seemingly occupied by their cell phones. "I shouldn't have walked away from you like that the other day."

"I get it. I really do. Can you spare five minutes over at the corner table?"

Estelle called out from the back room, "Yes, she can!"

Wolf winked. "Meet you there."

When Ivy arrived tableside, Wolf stood, pulled her close and kissed her. He nuzzled her cheek and said, "Had to do that. I missed it yesterday."

"I did, too. You must have been busy with work? To have missed your morning coffee?"

"I was. And… I wasn't sure you wanted to see me."

"Wolf, I always want to see you. We just…" She kissed his head then sat across from him at the small, intimate table. "I think we had our first fight the other day and I'm sorry."

"So am I. I promise that if it makes you upset when I offer money to you, I will never do it again. But, Ivy, can you trust me just a little? I'm a pretty smart guy. I know my reputation with women sucks, but—"

She leaned in to kiss him quickly, then said, "Yes. I trust you. It's been difficult for me to separate caring for my brother from having a life. But Ivan is a big boy. He's got this. And I realized that the having-a-life part is important for my mental health. And that ultimately makes me a better sister."

"Does the life you're talking about include a dorky coder with a penchant for death coffee?"

"It does. Can we kiss and make up after I get off work?"

"Deal."

Wolf's bedroom featured a massive paned window that overlooked an unkempt railyard. Lights strung along the pier beamed and flashed and twinkled like the stars Ivy missed.

"You never get to see stars when living in a big city," she said.

They'd just made love. Her body was lax and warm. Snuggled next to Wolf's warmth was the only place she wanted to be.

"You can see them in Burghausen."

"Is that where you intend to build your little cottage and raise a family?"

"There or somewhere in the vicinity. I like being close to a big city to access the things I need, but then to have the solace of a little town or village to keep my heart in place."

She turned and faced him. "Your heart belongs in Germany. Does this business thing in Venice have to do with you possibly moving back there someday?"

"It does. Concierge is moving to the next level. World domination!"

"And you plan to take over the world from a little village?"

"If I can, I will. I'm thinking of transferring control of the CEO duties to someone else and just becoming the owner who sits on the sidelines and oversees things."

"Wow. That's a huge step."

"It is, but more and more I believe it will make me happy."

"I can see that it will. I hope it all works out for you."

"It will if I can loosen my tight grip on the business reins. Now I'm going to ask you to Venice again and this time—"

"I'll go," she said simply. With a kiss and a nuzzle of her nose into his beard, she hugged up against his body. "I'd go anywhere with you, lover."

CHAPTER FIFTEEN

Venice

IVY HAD NEVER traveled out of the United States. Now, as Wolf helped her to step off the water taxi they'd taken from the Marco Polo Airport on the mainland over to the island of Venice, she took in everything. It was a completely different world from the tall buildings and enclosed tight spaces of New York. Water everywhere, and ancient buildings, and so many tourists bustling about. Wolf had insisted they do the tourist way of taking a taxi and walking to his palazzo instead of a private water taxi to his place. That way she could take in the Piazza San Marco and get a feel for the city before he had to leave her this afternoon for his meeting.

Following him through a bustle of sightseers, Ivy spread up her arms and tilted back her head. Everything smelled lush and like the sea. A green saltiness that she could literally taste at the back of her throat. When she walked right into Wolf, his grin was irrepressible.

"Penny for your thoughts? On the other hand, my money is no good to you so…just tell me what put that gorgeous smile on your face?"

"This place." She kissed him. And while he couldn't wrap his arms around her because he held both their suitcases, she pulled him in tight for a hug and another long kiss. "Thank you for convincing me to step out of my self-imposed boundaries. I know Ivan will be okay with Heather to watch him. And I intend to enjoy every moment I'm here."

"You don't know how happy that makes me. Come on. Let's do the fast and furious tour through the city. My place is a ten-minute walk from here."

They strolled through the massive Piazza San Marco, Wolf pointing out the Basilica that gleamed like a gold idol in the sunlight. The tall, bronze-capped Campanile that was once a beacon for incoming ships. And pigeons flying everywhere in wait of a dropped treat. The coming and going tides shushed a quiet symphony over the city. It was beautiful and such a wonder.

As they passed luxury storefronts, Ivy's head turned at the sight of a pretty red silk dress. Once again she walked right into Wolf.

He laughed and noticed what he drawn her attention. "F80825 is definitely your color."

"A color similar to the red velvet mite."

He hugged her. "We have our own unique languages but somehow we understand each other."

"I love your color language. I know your eyes are 724717. So! I feel like I need to buy myself a treat while I'm here," she said as they continued to walk. "Something small. A reminder of my visit."

"There're plenty of tourist shops. I'm sure you'll find something. Over there. That little restaurant looks unimpressive, but it has the best carbonara in the world. I'll take you there tonight."

"I look forward to it. Do you think I'll be okay to wander around on my own while you're at work?"

"Of course. Venice is a very walkable city. Let's sync our phones so if you do get lost, I can find you." He winked then nodded to the right. "Over here's my place."

The Istrian stone front of the palazzo was simple and unimposing. Wolf punched in the digital code and pushed the door open, allowing Ivy to walk in onto the marble-tiled floor that stretched to the opposite side of the building, where a tall doorway gated with wrought-iron let in the bright sun through colored glass. An old iron chandelier hung in the center of the long hall. To each side were doorways leading to rooms and places she was eager to discover.

"This is beautiful," she said. She rushed forward to look through the far doorway. The Veneto sloshed right up to a short dock and to the right she could see the open garage where boats must park. "Can we ride a gondola?"

"Yes, to everything you desire." Wolf set down the suitcases and pulled her into a long, soul-shivering hug. "You give the best hugs. I'm glad this place makes you happy."

"Being here with you is what makes me happy. But how soon before you abandon me?"

He checked his watch. "Actually, sooner than I thought. I have to meet the client in an hour. Time enough to take a shower and get on my way."

"Can I help with…" Ivy fluttered her lashes, not even embarrassed at such a cliché flirtation "…anything?"

He grabbed her hand, then with a fast move she didn't see coming, he swept her into his arms and carried her up a stairway. And Ivy recalled the day she and Estelle had made their lists of the perfect man. Sweeping a girl off her feet and up the stairs? Check *strong* off the list.

The only thing that remained was…believing in love.

And she wasn't so sure Wolf believed in that.

Ivy spent the afternoon walking the city. She strolled across bridges over canals and took in the opulent palazzos. Gondolas in all shapes, sizes and colors ferried sightseers along the waterways. Elaborate masks displayed in shop fronts drew her interest, and she watched one being crafted with feathers and rhinestones. She noshed on a Chantilly-cream-stuffed croissant, fried calamari, and tart lemon gelato. Window-shopping, she spied fabulous gowns, sky-high heels, pricey purses, and… She settled for a touristy T-shirt.

When she returned to the palazzo, she met Wolf as he was getting in. They kissed all the way across the threshold and halfway down the foyer.

"Did you have a good meeting?" she asked.

"Phenomenal. Concierge is going meta by the end of this year. It's going to be amazing, and take a lot of work, but the crew I spoke with today have already got people and projects set up to make it run smoothly. What about you? How was your day?"

"Perfect. A little lonely, but I only thought of you, hmm…a couple times an hour."

"Only a couple?"

"Well, I had to focus or walk into the Veneto! What's that you have behind your back? That pink bag does look intriguing."

"F808C4 is definitely another of your colors." He handed her the bag. "A treat for you. And I won't accept any arguments against it," he said as she pulled out the box from a clothing store.

"You won't get any." Ivy peeked in the box to see red silk. "The dress?"

"Yep. The store clerk wondered what size you wore and when I started to look around for a woman about your shape, I mentioned the dress had made you crash into me earlier. She saw that! And she said this would fit you perfectly."

"Will it be too fancy to wear out?"

"Never."

"Okay, give me ten minutes. I have to refresh from the day."

"Take all the time you like. But if you hear something rumbling down here," he called as she rushed up the stairs to the upper bedroom that overlooked the lagoon, "it's my stomach!"

Ten minutes later Ivy twisted her hair into a chignon and stuck a silver hair stick in to secure it. She stepped back and admired the dress in the floor-length mirror in the massive bathroom. The sensuous red silk landed just below her knees and swished with every move. It revealed every line, curve and indent on her body. The silk swept over one shoulder where a small gold ring connected the back to the front. The magnetic ring held a pouf of red silk at the top of her shoulder like a flower burst. It was a removable decoration. She liked it so she kept it on.

Who would have thought she'd be standing in Venice, wearing a beautiful dress given to her by her super-sexy, kind, handsome—and rich—boyfriend? Life could not get better. Well, it could, but she'd promised herself not to think about Ivan's troubles this weekend. She was in Venice! And the only dream she'd ever had of an overseas excursion had involved her dressed in khakis and wielding a mosquito net, searching for some rare insect to study.

She'd netted the best prize yet.

"Ivy!"

"I'm coming! Tell your stomach to hold on."

She hadn't a purse, so she slipped into the black heels she'd packed. An inch heel; perfect for walking. Sailing down the stairs, she saw Wolf had put on a suit coat and—oh, that dark beard and his piercing eyes always ignited her core. She landed in his arms and kissed him.

"That dress is…" He made a show of looking her over. "Not right."

"What?" Her shoulders dropped. She smoothed

a hand up her stomach. "But I thought you liked me in this hex code?"

"I love you in it. There's just something not right about that thing…" He pointed at her shoulder where the flower pouf sat.

"I can take it off. It's magnetic."

"I know." He grabbed the pouf of silk and tossed it over his shoulder. Then he pulled a small box out from inside his coat. "Got you something to replace it."

"Oh, Wolf, you didn't have—" Ivy stopped herself from refusing his kindness. She knew it came from his heart. "I love surprises. What is it?" She opened the flat box to discover a gorgeous brooch.

"I saw it in a jewelry store," he said. "I knew who it belonged to right away."

"This is incredible." The box dropped to the floor as she took out the brooch. It was a beetle, and the shell was metallic violet and red and green that changed with movement. "It looks like a *coleoptera buprestidae*. A jewel beetle. It's found on a small Indonesian island," she said. "I can't believe you found something like this." She turned it over to see it did not have a pin on the back of it but rather a small metal circle. "I'm not sure how to wear it, though."

"I asked the jeweler if he could make a specific adjustment." Wolf took the brooch from her. "And he had to do it in the few hours I was in the meeting. He stepped up to the challenge. So let's see if it works." He placed the beetle over the gold circle on her shoulder and it clicked into place.

"Oh my gosh!" Ivy rushed up to the massive mirror hung over a table on the opposite wall and studied the pin sitting on her shoulder as if the beetle had landed there. "It's perfect!" A giddy wave made her spin and do a little shimmy before dancing up to Wolf and hugging him. "I…" The words *love you* stalled on her tongue. Would they frighten him away? Did they frighten her? Best to avoid that truth at the moment. "Thank you, lover."

After dinner of fresh seafood and peach Moscato, Wolf escorted Ivy on a gondola ride in the San Polo, explaining that if they chose a less touristy canal the experience would be more romantic. Then he laughed at himself as he helped her step down into the gondola. Had he actually used the word *romantic*? Yes, yes, he had. And he looked forward to this moonlit ride upon the quiet, dark waters snuggled next to his girl.

Was he turning into some kind of romance hero? Crazy. The heroes always won the girl by the last page. He had even begun to dare to dream about his future. He'd dropped his caution when with Ivy. And it felt amazing.

Ivy settled into the plush red seat and leaned over the side to trail her fingers in the water. They glided down the narrow canal lit by festive lights that wrapped the few trees and many of the palazzo facades.

"Cold?" he asked.

"No, it's actually lukewarm."

"I mean you." He put an arm around her shoulder as she sat back and flicked the water from her fingers. "So what kinds of bugs would an entomologist find here in Venice?"

"On my walk I discovered a few private and public gardens humming with insects. Of course, there's mosquitoes. They love the water. I've never been a mosquito magnet."

"Me as well. So we're safe then." He kissed her and she turned her body to snuggle against his chest, but then she suddenly pointed upward.

"Look at that architecture!"

"I think that's a church. I haven't taken much time to sightsee Venice."

"But you have a home here."

"It's a stopover for when I'm in Europe. Also, when I started to grow my bank account it was a whim buy. I liked the idea of owning a palazzo."

"I can't imagine buying something on a whim

beyond some pretty shoes or a fancy chocolate bar. You could rent it out when you're not here?"

"I could but…it's mine. I don't like people touching my things. And to know strangers were actually living in my home?" He mocked a shudder.

"Does that come from you growing up in foster homes? Not having much to call your own?"

She was perceptive. "It does. I suppose I'd never make a good client for one of your brother's house-sitting jobs, eh? What do you think about that sunset?"

She tilted her head against his shoulder and slid a hand over his chest. They snuggled and watched as the boat sailed closer to the end of the canal that opened onto the Grand Canal, which Wolf had instructed the gondolier to take to his palazzo.

This was a dream. Because he'd allowed himself to drop his caution, he now sat next to a woman he cared about. Wolf wasn't sure when he'd last felt so unencumbered. His shoulders relaxed even more. So many things left his muscle memory with a sigh. To be replaced with the happiness of simply being.

"I'm glad you convinced me to come along with you to Venice," she said. "This is an experience I won't forget."

He nuzzled his nose aside her luscious locks,

kissing her head. "Being with you makes me forget everything to do with the rush-rush of business. You calm me, Ivy. I've never felt this way with another person."

"Maybe it's that I bore you?" She popped up her head to meet his gaze. The fairy lights strung along the windows of the homes they passed glittered in her eyes.

"Never," he breathed and then bowed to kiss her. But it was an abrupt one.

"It feels weird to kiss with the gondolier right there."

Wolf smirked against her mouth. "He's seen it before."

"Still, let's save it for when we get to the palazzo."

She was a private person, and more power to her. So Wolf would not point out the paparazzi he spied in the gondola across the canal. How did they always find him? Probably they'd been tracking him since he'd arrived this morning. And with those long-range lenses they surely got the shot. Had they snapped one of them kissing?

The tension that had sluiced from his veins scurried back through his system, as he kept one eye on the photogs and directed the gondolier to his private dock. When they arrived, he leaped out to help Ivy from the gondola. The photographers yelled across the canal for them to pose. They also called out, asking if they were a couple.

"I didn't even see them," Ivy said as she ducked behind him.

He could feel her tremble. And that stirred his rage. He fisted a nasty gesture to the photographers and called out an oath—the only one he knew in Italian—then grabbed Ivy's hand and pulled her inside the palazzo, slamming the door behind him.

A search light from the photographer's boat flashed through the windows. His hand turned the knob, but he didn't open the door. That's what they wanted from him. To see him react. To get salacious photos to smear all over some social media page.

So much for dropping his caution.

"I'm sorry." He leaned his head against the door and splayed out his arms. "I shouldn't have done that. I thought I was better at ignoring them."

"Don't apologize. It's rude that they think they can intrude on your life like that."

It was, and yet...

"Yes, but I just broke a rule," he said. "There's a certain social contract. A quid pro quo. It's expected that, as a celebrity, I will allow the press to report on me, take photos, and print them.

And as long as I play along, they'll be kind, or at the very least, print the photos where I'm not stuffing my face with food. But when I turn on them, as I did just now, then they'll punish me with bad press. It's how the game is played."

"But when did you agree to play such a ridiculous game? It's not fair."

"It's not, but that's how it works. I'm sorry."

"Don't apologize anymore. And thank you for schooling me on the rules. It was a few seconds. Forgotten. In the past." She lifted her chin and looked at him through long, lush lashes. "I want to play a different game."

With that, she took off the magnetic bug pin from her dress and turned to walk toward the stairs. Slipping the gold ring and red fabric from her shoulder, she cast him a teasing look and a blown kiss. Then she dashed up the stairs.

Wolf caught that kiss right in his heart. It went in smooth as an arrow, but he didn't feel any pain. Only a hot explosion of desire. He flicked the lock on the door behind him, then raced up the stairs.

CHAPTER SIXTEEN

"DID YOU KNOW there is a research institute on the mainland that is scheduled to do a study on damselflies?"

Ivy sat up straight from her slumped position on a bench. After a late breakfast, they'd walked for hours, then found a sunny spot in the Campo Santa Maria Formosa to rest. The bench was backed by a thick jasmine hedge, and the scent intoxicated. Wolf had been occupied with his phone for twenty minutes, which she knew was probably work, but she didn't mind.

"How do you know that?" she asked.

He turned his phone toward her. The screen showed a website for an Italian institute that listed a call for entomologists. He'd been researching jobs for her while she'd been aimlessly watching tourists? What a sweet move.

"You should apply," he said. "You'd probably get the job. It starts next year."

The project did sound interesting. And to work

in Venice? And to actually hold a real job in her field and not have to sling lattes and mocha loca whatevers?

Ivy's shoulders slumped and she shook her head. "I'd love to, but Ivan still isn't in a place where he can manage on his own."

"Ivy, Ivan has help."

"We can't expect Heather to be a girlfriend and a full-time caregiver. That's asking far too much."

"So, you'll hire a different nurse for your brother. If he even requires one. And it's still half a year away. Ivy, this is a challenge I'm issuing you. Like a calendar page."

"That's a whole lot bigger than a suggestion to eat lemon cake. Ivan needs me."

Wolf sighed heavily and leaned back, their shoulders hugging. "The last time I brought this up you walked away from me so I'm a little leery, but…"

Yes, she did have a tendency to run when confronted with truths she didn't like to face. The man did not deserve that from her. It was about time she pulled up her big girl panties and faced reality. Life was difficult. Dealing with it required finesse. And she was a woman who possessed finesse and determination. Time to stop reacting.

"Say it."

With a heavy sigh, he then asked, "Is it that Ivan needs you, or that you need to *feel needed* by him?"

Was it? No, it—well, there were many other factors. She would step away and start her own life as soon as she felt confident Ivan had a handle on his situation. It would happen. And her brother would never ask her to stay longer than she was needed.

And…yes. She did like to feel needed.

But also, she'd realized he could take care of his issues on his own. So what excuses had she left?

"And I'm not going to accept the money argument," Wolf added. "There are foundations, charities, grants that Ivan can apply for. I know, because I've done the research."

"You have?"

He nodded. "I did some research on the flight here while you were sleeping. I also worked on my newest project."

She had slept six hours and didn't even feel jet lag. But she'd been unaware he had been awake the whole time. Did the man never sleep? "A new project?"

"It was inspired by your brother's condition. It's a medical labeling app that puts QR codes on all prescriptions. Users scan the code before taking the medication. They can set the app to speak the medication name out loud so they can confirm it's correct, and even use the camera to identify the pills by shape and color. It should reduce mistakes measurably. I've already tasked someone at Concierge with taking charge of the project."

"That's incredible. And sounds very usable. I wish Ivan had such a thing days ago. You really do care about people."

"Don't let anyone know. I might get a complex."

The man was a wonder. And seeing this charitable side of him made her fall even deeper in love than she already was. Yes, she loved Wolf. But she still didn't dare tell him.

"Listen, Ivy." He kissed the back of her hand. "I respect your need to take care of your brother, to ensure he gets the very best care. But you can't do for your brother unless you take care of yourself."

Her thoughts, exactly. Why did she find it easier to believe coming from him and not her own thoughts?

"You've got to make yourself happy. I'm not asking you to take my money. I'm just asking you to trust that Ivan will find his way through this."

"I understand. To be honest? I do like the feeling of being needed. Yet, I really do want to be working in my field. But that Venice study is a long way from New York."

"What if Ivan got accepted into a research study somewhere in Europe?"

"We did fill out an application for a study in Sweden. He qualifies. But if he did get accepted, his living expenses would not be paid. We've been living on the remainder of the sale from our parents' home. It may cover a stay in Sweden, but I haven't researched the expense side of it yet."

"Please reconsider my offer to pay Ivan's expenses. And…about allowing me to make that offer directly to Ivan. It is his life, after all. And you know I'm not doing this as a means to buy your love, right?"

Soft brown eyes searched hers with a glint of hope. Of course, she knew that. He wasn't the kind of person who could even think to buy her love. Albeit, he had used money to buy off bullies when he was a kid. That had been a survival reaction. A smart one, too. And his money wasn't offered to her as a means to silence her about faulty boat parts that had caused her parents' deaths. This was completely different. He just wanted to help Ivan get the best care.

"I'm just like you, Ivy." He tilted his head onto her shoulder. "I'm still that scrawny kid who is trying to navigate his way through life and be accepted by others. Somebody tossed a boatload of money at me, but it didn't change who I am inside. You have to believe that."

"I do believe that. I know you are kind and sweet and honest and… I feel as though I've been living in a fairy tale lately. I got to wear the gown to a fabulous ball. And my coach didn't even turn into a pumpkin. And now I've been taken to a kingdom of wonder by a handsome prince."

Wolf's look melted right into her heart. "You know this regular guy found a beautiful princess who wears bugs on her shoulder and beams like the sun. I'm the one who feels like a prince who won the best thing in the world."

"You won my heart the moment you said my name in But First…"

He gave her a wondering lift of brow and she nodded.

"I'll look up the application for the Venice study," she said. "And… I'll seriously consider applying."

"Yes!"

On the flight home, Wolf slipped into a snooze with the ease of closing his eyes. Ivy found that remarkable. With the time changes she'd experienced over the past few days, she was wide awake.

Fortunately, the in-flight Wi-Fi allowed her to do some surfing. She read all the details for the Venice study. It was right up her alley. It didn't begin until next March. Dare she apply for it? Surely that would allow ample time to get Ivan set on the right path and leave him feeling like he had a handle on the MS?

Why was she so determined to control Ivan's life? As Wolf had suggested, wasn't it Ivan's choice whether or not he accepted help from Wolf? It was his disease. She couldn't know his every thought, concern, or desire regarding how he wished to proceed with such a diagnosis. And she had gotten the feeling when talking to him about how he would answer if he had been offered money by Wolf that Ivan would say yes.

Perhaps it was time she surrendered to the universe and simply went along with it. Actually ask Ivan for his input instead of planning around him.

With a nod, she decided she would have a good talk with Ivan. Thanks to Wolf's influence, she was learning to relax a little, allow life to flow without feeling as though she had to stand and face it with a shield and sword. Everything was going to be okay.

Touching the insect pin made her smile. The jeweler had designed it so a magnetic piece holding a pin could be fitted into the back for when she didn't wear it on the red dress. Now it sat on the shoulder of her tee shirt just for fun.

She wanted to know more about the artist so she found the website and read up on the enameling process and how he crafted his insects based on real ones but added his own whimsical touches. With a click, her screen flashed with a bunch of obnoxious ads for celebrity sites. Finger hovering over the delete button, her vision focused on a shot of a familiar man, standing on a dock before a Venetian palazzo, giving the photographer a nasty gesture.

"Oh, dear."

The headline read: *Rogue Billionaire Shows His Ugly Side!*

Ivy quickly read the article below the image.

Tech billionaire Wolfgang Zeigler, on a trip to Venice with his latest paramour, explodes at photographers.

"He didn't explode," she muttered. "He had every right to be angry. They were using searchlights!"

The article continued.

Will this woman be like all the rest? Does Zeigler have a cool million set aside to as-

suage her shopping needs and head off a litigious attack?

Ivy's jaw dropped open. How dare they assume so much? It was completely untrue.
She read more.

According to an anonymous source, Zeigler now has all his dates vetted with a thorough background check. She must have passed!

Now Ivy's jaw snapped shut. She reread that line about the background check. Then she glanced to the sleeping billionaire beside her. Had Wolf had her checked out? How dare he? After their conversation about how a person should be allowed their privacy, and his fight to keep that...
She shook her head and flicked the screen off on her cell phone.
Under her breath she muttered, "Jerk."

CHAPTER SEVENTEEN

AFTER DEPLANING, and while waiting for their luggage, Wolf noticed Ivy's quiet mood. He kissed her on the forehead but didn't try to engage. She hadn't slept on the flight, so probably wanted to get home and crawl into bed.

She followed him to the curb where a limo waited and allowed him to open the back door for her and slide in beside her. But when he bent to kiss her, she turned her head and closed her eyes.

"Sorry," he said. "I get the jet lag thing. I'll have you home in no time so you can get some sleep."

She sighed and shook her head. "I'm not tired. Well, I am. I'm just…"

The limo pulled away from the curb. Ivy's hair was in a not-so-neat ponytail and her touristy T-shirt featuring a map of the Venetian lagoon was rumpled. The bug pin glinted on her shoulder. A beautiful mess. But Wolf could feel tension waver from her.

When she didn't seem to want to continue what she was saying, he leaned back and closed his eyes. The limo navigated the bustling New York expressways. Venice had been a treat. He'd never enjoyed himself with a woman so much. Not a thing about Ivy felt wrong.

Save for the chill vibes he was sensing from her now. What had he done wrong? He didn't want to do this again. Not when he'd thought they'd come to an agreement about silly arguments over silly things.

"What is it, Ivy? Talk to me."

With a heavy sigh she finally faced him. In a weary tone, she asked, "You did a check on me?"

"What?"

"I read an article about us on the flight. It posted the photo they took of us on the dock with you flipping them off. They mentioned something about the rogue billionaire doing a background check on all his girlfriends?"

Hell. So that was the press's punishment for his fit of anger? Touché. "Ivy, it's something my lawyer suggested I do after the lawsuit."

"You think I'm going to sue you? Take you for millions? My God, you know nothing about me."

"Ivy, I do know you. And I know you would never do anything like that. But…"

"But you still had a background check done on me?"

He nodded. "It's something I need to do to protect myself. Legally. Please believe me when I say I didn't read it."

"Why not?"

"Because you're different. You're… Ivy."

She shook her head. "I can't believe you would do such a thing."

The limo pulled over. They had arrived before Ivan's brownstone. She got out and slapped a hand on the trunk. The driver opened the trunk, and before Wolf could help her, she held her suitcase in hand.

"Let me help you with that, please."

"I don't want to talk to you right now." She tugged the wheeled suitcase toward the front of the brownstone.

Wolf splayed out his arms, at a loss at what to say or do. Whenever she was confronted by something she didn't like, she fled. Pushed him away. Like he wasn't important enough to stay and work things out.

And that hurt his heart so much, he clasped a hand over his chest. Ivy made him feel unworthy of her love.

Heather greeted Ivy when she got inside. The bubbly therapist asked all sorts of questions

CINDERELLA'S BILLION-DOLLAR INVITATION

about her trip. All Ivy wanted to do was bury her head under the sheets and cry. Wolf had betrayed her. In the cruelest manner.

Seeing her yawn, Heather said Ivan was showering and they intended to go for a walk in the park. Ivy said she needed some rest and thanked her.

It was six hours later when Ivy woke and pushed tangled hair from her face. Someone knocked on her bedroom door. Heather called softly, "Mr. Zeigler is here to see you."

She glanced to the bedside clock. Seven in the evening. Still out of it and feeling her anger rush up and warm her neck, Ivy said, "I don't want to talk to him. Tell him to go away."

After a long, restorative shower, she combed through her hair and decided her sleep schedule would force her to try and sleep again tonight if she wanted to adjust and make it to work in the morning. She was awake now and hungry. But hearing Ivan and Heather laughing out in the living room made her want to hide away. They sounded happy.

She had had such a wonderful time in Venice with Wolf. The prince had won her heart.

Only to crush it with a background check.

And while common sense prodded at her to view this from both sides, right now she was hurt and confused and…she glanced out the window overlooking the front sidewalk. She recognized the back of Wolf's head. He was sitting out on the park bench. Had he been sitting there since he'd knocked about an hour ago?

She pulled the curtain before the window. She didn't want to talk to him. Not yet.

"What are you doing?" she muttered. Hadn't she left her need to react in Venice? Wasn't she moving onward and upward, taking life at an easier pace?

Apparently not.

To distract her thoughts, she wandered out to the living room. Half a delivery pizza sat on the counter. Heather had also just popped popcorn and the rich buttery scent filled the room.

"We're going to watch *Princess Bride*," Heather said. "Want to join us?"

Ivy didn't want anything to do with fairy-tale love right now.

"He's still out there." Ivan glanced over the back of the couch out the front window. "You going to talk to him?"

She shook her head and took a big bite of pizza. Ugh. Cold pepperoni grease.

"It's not my place to ask what sort of romantic squabble the two of you are entangled in," Ivan said, "but I suspect the guy might sit out there all night. And it's starting to rain."

Ivan could ask her whatever he wished. Because she had swept in and taken charge of his life...

Ivy swallowed hard on a bite of pizza. Had she ever really asked Ivan what *he* wanted, how he wanted to proceed forward? Or had she literally moved in, made up lists of studies and doctors and taken over his life?

"I'm sorry," she said to her brother. "I really am."

He didn't hear her as the opening music for the movie started.

Outside, raindrops spattered the window. Ivy dropped the half slice on the greasy cardboard and then went to face her demons. By the time she got to the park bench, rain beaded her hair. Her bare toes squished in the grass.

Wolf stood as she rounded the bench. "I'm sorry, Ivy."

"You shouldn't be sitting out in the rain. You'll catch a cold."

"That's an old wives' tale."

Likely. But how to start this conversation she didn't want to have but really needed to have?

"I just wanted to make sure you were okay," he said. Then with a heavy sigh, he added, "You pushed me away, Ivy. Do you know how that makes me feel?"

She did. Because he'd shared that personal part of his growing up. How cruel of her to have ignored his feelings for her own stupid anger. An anger she had once already chastised herself for allowing to react when it wasn't fair to him.

"I've lived that all my life. I won't do it anymore." He tugged a manila envelope out of his jacket and handed it to her. "The flash drive is in there. My guy never emails me info. Too easy to trace. The envelope is still sealed. I didn't open it. I…should have never done it, but it's what I've been conditioned to do. I know that's not fair to you."

She took the envelope, which was getting wetter by the second, and tucked it under her T-shirt.

"I wish I could take it back," he said. "But it's who and what I am. I protect my boundaries."

But he had let her inside those boundaries. And she had banged against them and kicked in a few holes. Politely, and…very well, those angry outbursts had been undeserved.

"I know it's going to be a barrier to me ever finding someone to love me," he said. "But I don't believe in love anyway. I want to believe in it, but I know if I do, it'll be ripped away from me. So there you go."

Ivy's heart dropped. He didn't believe in love. And yet…

Wolfgang Zeigler just didn't know what love

felt like and so when he found it, he couldn't recognize it.

"I hope you'll call me after looking through the information on that drive," he said. "But if you don't, I guess I'll have to accept that."

He kissed her forehead. "I..." Another heavy sigh. What was it he wanted to say but couldn't?

With that, he walked away.

Rain blended with Ivy's teardrops. She had hurt that man as much as he had hurt her. But *had* he hurt her? He hadn't even looked at the information on the flash drive.

Why couldn't she make herself run after him, call the prince back into her life?

Because maybe this makeshift princess didn't deserve such a wonderful man.

CHAPTER EIGHTEEN

ON WEDNESDAY, Wolf's calendar suggested he learn a few words in a new language. Thirty-four hours had passed since he'd spoken to Ivy. In the rain. And his heart felt as if it still rained within. She'd not contacted him. Which meant she didn't want anything to do with him. He'd avoided going into But First... for both their sakes.

He'd been honest with her. And yet, he knew part of what he'd said had been a lie. He really did want to believe in love. And he may have found it. Was it love? He'd never felt so torn over a woman. But if this was love, now it was too late to keep it.

He grabbed the calendar and flung it across the office. It hit the wall and the plastic frame broke. Pages scattered on the floor.

Ivy filled an order for six lattes, each involving various complicated recipes, and put the cups in a cardboard carrier and handed it to the perky

young accountant who came in every morning
to fill her office order. With Estelle out talking
to a new vendor, she and Valerie were left to
manage the lunch rush.

She appreciated the busyness. Otherwise, her
mind would switch to everything she'd discovered on that stupid flash drive. The envelope
had indeed still been sealed. Though she had
mentally argued that Wolf could have put it in a
new one after opening it, she reasoned his word
had always been good.

What the background check contained had
startled her. Made her angry. And then made
her cry. So much information! Most of it in-
nocuous. Yet, that a private detective had found
out so much about her life frightened her. It
listed her addresses since childhood. All jobs,
all schools and even college tuition charges.
Where she shopped and how often she'd hit the
fast food drive-thru in her hometown. All of it
trackable with a credit card, she realized. It included various websites she had browsed, the
number of calls she made to hospitals and clin-
ics on Ivan's behalf.

But worst? It had listed the information on her
parents' deaths and included the details on the
settlement she and Ivan had refused. The information came from the boat company and had

labeled them as insurance frauds. Seriously? As if she and her brother were the criminals!

She'd pulled the flash drive from her laptop and tossed it across the room.

"Ivy, did you get the Americano for the gentleman in the red shirt?" Valerie called.

Right. Clear her brain of that horrifying report and get to work. Focus!

She tilted a double shot of finely ground beans into the portafilter and tamped it, then slid it into the espresso machine. Looking over the top of the machine, she zoomed in on the front door. He hadn't come in on Tuesday, or today. Hadn't even sent someone down for coffee and his chocolate chip cake.

Was he avoiding her? Or was he simply done with her?

She didn't want either. She probably deserved both.

She had to make things right.

Around six, Ivy finally punched out. She'd been in the shop since seven a.m. Had gotten a half hour lunch break. Estelle had issues with a few vendors and hadn't been able to come in at all. Ivy hadn't minded the double shift, but now she was tired. Perhaps some jet lag still lingered. Or maybe it was that she wasn't right with the world. Things had changed between her and

Wolf. But that didn't mean those changes had to tear them apart. She didn't want that. They needed to talk.

Out front of But First..., she paused and looked to the left where the main entry doors for the building were located. Most of the Concierge office had likely punched out, but Wolf tended to work until something compelled him to stand and shake out his muscles.

She turned and walked by the gym that required a membership and code to get in—she raced up to the door just as the woman she recognized as the receptionist walked out. Over her head, she could see Wolf inside, lifting weights.

"Could I...slip inside?" she asked sweetly. "My boyfriend is back there."

The woman nodded and opened the door for her. "He's a nice catch."

He was. But did she still have control of the net? She had to stop thinking in such terms. The man was free, and no one had a right to *net* him.

Ivy slipped inside and strolled past a few stationary bicycles, some rowers, and stacks of weights. A boxing ring sat at the back of the club. It smelled like a sweaty gym, but the alluring scent that drew her like a moth to a flame was just a few steps away.

As she gained his side, Wolf noticed her and

set down the weights labeled with a fifty on each. "Ivy?"

"Can we talk?"

He grabbed a white towel and swiped it over his face. "Yes."

He gestured she sit on a chair near the boxing ring, but she declined, so he punched a nearby heavy bag a couple times, then swung around to face her. "Did you read the report?"

"I did. And I believe that you did not since the envelope was still sealed."

"I couldn't." He approached her and took her hands. She wanted to lunge against him and hug him forever. That good hug that only they shared. But this talk was necessary. "The day I got that report I should have tossed it. I knew then I'd never look at it."

She exhaled and nodded. "I'm not mad at you. I swear I'm not. Well, I was initially. But now that I've had some time to think about it, there's not a thing that you did wrong. You do need to protect yourself. Because of your job and your finances, it's a smart thing to do. I get that."

"Doesn't make it a good thing."

She nodded in agreement. "I'm more angry now because of all the information contained in the report. I don't understand how anyone can have so much of my personal and private information."

"Ivy, it's all data. The thing any company would pay big bucks for. Data that's gathered through every means possible. Every application you fill out. Every financial transaction. Every text, every message, every email you send."

"It's—it can't be legal."

He shook his head. "Do you ever read the terms and conditions? No one does. It's how companies cover their asses and give themselves access to anything and everything you put out there. I'm sorry."

"So a person can never have a completely private life?"

"You can if you stop using cell phones and apps."

"But I..." She took out her cell phone and stared at it. "I guess I know that nothing is secure or safe. We're all deceiving ourselves by thinking otherwise. Damn it." She opened the screen and clicked on the Concierge app. With one press of her finger she deleted it.

Wolf watched from beside her. "That's a good start."

"Seriously? You don't mind me tossing your app? You're contributing to the data mining with this app."

"I know. And again, it's all in the terms and conditions. Everyone knows they are handing over their personal information for the use of a convenience. It's a choice they make."

"That's not untrue. God, I hate this."

"If you're serious about protecting your privacy I can help you, but it'll require a tech sabbatical."

"I don't need Concierge. I just like the convenience, as you've said. I'm sure there's lots of apps I don't need. I can't think of one that is necessary. But my phone can still be tracked. They had locations on that report. It was creepy."

"Listen, this is a whole big conversation that I want to have with you. I'd love to teach you how to protect your privacy. But what I really want to know right now is…"

She kissed him. It had been almost two days since she'd last tasted him, felt his rugged physique meld against her, touched his warm skin. Entered that space that only they shared. A space so vast and yet cozy at the same time.

"Can you forgive me for the way I reacted to all this?" she asked.

"You don't need forgiveness, Ivy. I understand your reaction. I really do."

"But I hurt you. Treated you like…" He hadn't been worthy of a calm and rational approach to the information he'd given her.

"I know it wasn't malicious."

"You were just trying to protect yourself. And

I want you to know there's nothing about me that I wouldn't share with you. You can have the flash drive back."

"I don't want it. Anything I learn about you I want to learn directly from you."

"Same. I don't want to believe anything about you that's been printed in a celebrity rag. I understand now why a little cottage in Germany appeals so much to you. Will you take me to Burghausen someday? I'd like to visit the place that gives you such wonderful memories."

"Really? Does that mean...?"

"What? Do you think we won't have the occasional argument? I'm still in if you are."

"Ah, hell yes."

He lifted her and as she glided lower in his embrace their mouths met and she wrapped her legs about his hips to stay there. Only his. She loved this man.

Two days later, Wolf looked up from coding as his office door opened and in walked Ivy all smiles and coffee and cake.

"Hey." He pushed back in his chair. A glance to the clock on the computer screen showed just before ten. "But First... has started delivery?"

"Only for our most handsome customers." She set the provisions on his desk then walked around to kiss him. The office walls were glass, so anyone walking by could see them. The kiss was too quick, but office compliant. "I have good news and couldn't wait to tell you about it."

"What's up?"

"Ivan got accepted into the Swedish study and it starts next month!"

He stood and pulled her into a hug. It was an easy reaction. "I'm happy for him. That's amazing."

"Yes, and he asked Heather to go along with him and she's in. And you know, it won't be as expensive as I'd expected. Well, he'll have to pay rent, but they've already sent info on rentals close to the study facility. And he'll have to cover food and other things. But the medical care is completely covered, and it includes physical and mental health checks. It sounds perfect for him."

"It does. But I suspect that'll set the two of you back, no matter how much you say it won't?"

She shrugged. "We'll deal. And we talked to the owners of the brownstone this morning. They agreed to allow me to stay on to complete Ivan's contract through January. I'll start looking for jobs this winter."

Wolf should feel buoyed by her enthusiasm. And he did. So why did he feel as though she was pushing him away by not asking him for financial assistance? Surely, the move would tax the Quinns' wallets. And Heather was going along too? A trip across the ocean, with an extended stay, would not be cheap.

"You don't seem excited?" Her shoulders wilted. "I'm bugging you, aren't I? You were probably immersed in an important project—"

Deciding a kiss was the easiest way to waylay her concerns, he pulled her close and initiated the distraction. Ivy had succeeded in what she'd come to New York to do. Help her brother move forward. And even though she would still be in the city through most of the winter, eventually she'd leave.

Would she walk away from him as well?

Ivy pulled away from the kiss and her eyes darted back and forth between his. "Something isn't right?"

He exhaled. "Sorry. No, everything is as you deserve. I'm just…like you said, I was coding and sometimes I'm so deep in it that it just takes me a while to come back to the normal world."

"I know that about you." She kissed him on the nose. "And I'm not going to hang around any longer and give your office mates something to gossip about. Just wanted to bring you fuel and tell you the great news. Call me later?"

"Absolutely."

With one more kiss, she left, walking by his office with a wave and a bounce to her step.

Wolf leaned forward, palms to the desk. The coffee smelled strong. The cake sat inside a neatly folded packet. A beautiful, smart, funny woman loved him. Everything was perfect.

So why did he feel as though her not asking him for money had been the hardest hit he'd ever taken? He wasn't that guy anymore. The kid who had to buy off the bullies. The man who had to flash his credit card to feel validated by others. All he'd wanted was freedom from the chains of his billions. And now that he'd found that freedom, he couldn't help but toe those chains and wonder what the hell was wrong with him.

"Nothing. Maybe."

He shook his head. Why was this so difficult to just allow to happen? Ivy and Ivan had a handle on things.

You can make it easier for them.

Did he need to do what he was thinking about doing? It would upset Ivy, surely. But…he had to give it a try. Not because he wanted to buy her love. He had that. He simply wanted to show the Quinn siblings how much he cared about them. And there was only one way he knew how to do that.

It would be a risk. He could lose Ivy in the process.

"I have to try."

* * *

It was after four when Ivy punched out at But First… She swung around the corner of the building, heading for the main entrance, knowing Wolf would still be sitting behind his desk. The man worked too much. She certainly hoped, now that she had begun to solidify her future, that she could encourage him to make some changes. Perhaps even look into moving and taking a smaller role in his company so he could have more time for life. And her.

Janice held the door for her, nodding and then calling after her as she entered, "Wolf isn't in there! He left about an hour ago."

"Oh." Ivy turned and the woman still held the door open for her. He'd left early and hadn't even stopped into the shop?

"Everything okay?" Janice asked.

"Of course. I must have forgotten he had plans. Thanks for saving me a trip in the elevator. You have a good afternoon." She walked onward, sensing the woman wanted to chat. To dig up some gossip? Likely.

She walked quickly, but her pace slowed as she got closer to the brownstone. Tugging out her phone, she texted Wolf to see if he wanted to get something to eat. He didn't answer, which worried her.

Had she read him incorrectly this morning?

She'd sensed something hadn't been right, that he'd not been as excited about her news as expected. Had it been more than her disturbing his work? Did he think this meant she was leaving him after the brownstone owners returned early next year?

That was half a year away. And she certainly hoped their relationship had more staying power than that. On the other hand, she knew his dating history. He was not a man who seemed to prefer settling in happily ever after.

What was she thinking? Her relationship with him was different. It had staying power. They cared about each other. Loved…

He didn't believe in love. Had never received it his entire life, so how could he really recognize it when he did receive it from her? Had she shown him her heart? Was he capable of moving beyond his emotional traumas to embrace what she wanted to wholeheartedly give him?

With tears spilling down her cheeks, she sniffed them away as she met Heather and Ivan outside the brownstone door. "Heading out for a walk?"

"We're going for dinner," Ivan said with a wave of his cane. "Celebrating."

"Of course! You're looking rather steady tonight."

"I feel incredible."

"I think the good news is a balm," Heather added. "He's been pacing and jumping. It's exciting."

"You two have fun. I'll see you later."

"Tell Wolf thanks again," Ivan said as the twosome walked down the steps, slowly, but with a steadiness that Ivy noticed.

"Thanks?" Ivy stepped inside and walked down the hallway to the kitchen, where she found Wolf sitting at the counter nursing a lemonade. "Hi. What brings you here? And why does Ivan want me to offer you thanks?"

He patted the stool beside him and she sat. He took her hand and kissed it. "I did something."

"A good something?"

"I think it is. But you might not."

Her heart dropped. This was it. The big goodbye. She'd been wondering if he was capable of allowing her into his heart and— But really? No. There was only one thing that the two of them didn't agree on, and that was money. She drew in a breath and cautioned herself from reacting. She didn't want to do that with him. Not anymore.

"I'm sorry for the way I acted this morning," he said. "I guess some feelings and emotions are still deeply embedded inside me. It'll take a while to move beyond."

Beyond what? The need to protect his heart? "I don't want to guess at what you're implying."

"Honestly? I was hurt when you didn't ask me for money to fund your brother's adventure."

"Oh." As she'd suspected.

"And I reasoned with myself. I know I shouldn't be hurt, and that you didn't intend it that way, but that stupid little kid inside of me eventually won out. I know that the two of you have got this. I also know that you don't want to take money from me, and it's not because of pride but simply because, well…"

"It's a little bit of pride." She slid her fingers along his and lifted his hand to press aside her cheek. "But as I've realized, it's not even my choice, is it?"

"It's not. Which means… I offered Ivan a small stipend to get him through a year or so in Sweden." He winced, waiting for her reaction.

Was that it? Mercy, she'd never been more relieved. Ivy bowed her forehead to his. "Thank you."

He tilted up her face with a touch to her chin. "That's it?"

She nodded.

"No argument?"

She shook her head.

"But I thought… And you know, I know that if I'm ever going to get beyond this need to feel, well…needed, I've got to stop handing out money. But. Another part of me just wanted to help. And who better to help than a family I genuinely care about?"

"Who indeed? I completely relate to your wanting to feel needed. We both know I've struggled with the same." She kissed him. "Thank you. I'm sure Ivan is grateful. As am I."

"That was easier than I'd expected. I thought we'd have an argument."

"I don't want to argue with you, Wolf. I want to love you. But there's one thing…" She bracketed her hands aside his head to study his eyes. So kind and smart and funny. Love was easy when in his arms. "It was something you said. It was a lie. But I don't think you realize that."

"What did I say?"

"You said you didn't believe in love."

He nodded. When his smile grew, her heart pulsed tentatively.

"I'm pretty sure it wasn't a lie. At the time," he said. "I've never felt worthy of love, Ivy. But you have changed the way I think. Made it possible to step beyond what I've known and look to what is possible. Love is…trust and respect and desire and sex and talking out arguments and even sharing food and a secret color language?"

He got it. Oh, did he get it.

"I love you," Ivy rushed out, tears spilling from her eyes. "And I see you. I see the little boy who never felt he was lovable enough to be kept by a family. And I see the man who just wants to be normal and learn how to live in a world that expects so much from him. I choose you to be a part of my life and my family. I love you, Wolf."

"I love you, Ivy. And the way I feel right now? My heart is thundering and my gut is spinning, but my body is chill and like, yeah, this is what it's like. Like going on the best ride you've ever taken. So that's love, eh?"

"It is. Will you take me on that ride with you?"

"Hell, yes."

EPILOGUE

One year later...

IVY HUGGED UP against Wolf, clasped his hand, and kissed him. He looked sexy in a tuxedo. And she was wearing the red dress he'd bought for her in Venice. He'd needed to look dapper. As Ivan's best man, Wolf had stepped up.

The wedding was held in an outdoor chapel not far from the Swiss village where Ivan and Heather now lived. Petite cornflowers decorated the simple altar and the bride's bouquet. Thanks to some of the health measures Ivan had learned while in the study, he had greatly improved his condition. But he still had a journey ahead of him, incorporating the disease into the adventurous lifestyle that gave him breath and happiness. He and Heather would begin an across-the-world adventure in a few weeks. And he had planned to document his experience as it unfolded in an online memoir. Ivy felt sure he would accomplish everything he desired.

After a stint working on the research study in Venice last fall and winter, Ivy had recently been accepted to head a study on butterflies in the rainforest. That project began in a month. And she was so ready!

Wolf was excited for her, but had pushed ahead the building project for his home in Burghausen by months in order to occupy it himself while she was away for work. He intended to fly to the Amazon for visits. She wouldn't have it any other way.

"Let's walk." Wolf nodded toward a crushed stone path that edged the woods hugging the venue. He tugged at his blue tie, loosening it. "Maybe you'll catch a bug or two?"

Ivy set her champagne goblet on the tray of a passing waiter, and with a wink to her brother, she strolled off with the man of her dreams. A man who had learned over the course of their relationship that he actually did believe in love.

She'd known as much all along. And he was strong and smart and capable of carrying her through thick and thin. He was her rock. And he ticked off every item on her list. Ha! That list. She had not made it thinking it would actually come to fruition. Guess fairy tales really did come true.

As for her field notes on the species *wolfus zeiglerus*, they would never end. Always she was learning something new about him and hoped it would continue.

"I'm not sure about this trip to the Amazon," she suddenly blurted out as they strolled along the tree line.

"What?" He stopped and leaned against a rustic wooden fence post. "Are you telling me you don't want to fulfill your dream of finding the blushing phantom butterfly?"

He remembered that was one of her dreams. God, did she love this man!

"Of course, I do. It's just that we'll be away from each other for three months. I wish I could stick you in my backpack and take you along."

"I did say I'd visit every other weekend."

"I know. And I will count the days between those visits." A kiss was necessary. And another. He slid a hand along her neck and pulled her in for a deeper connection. She melted against him. No place she'd rather be. "I love you."

"I love you as much as you love butterflies."

"Wow."

"That's a lot, isn't it?" he said with a grin.

"So much."

"Wait a second…" He reached over her shoulder. "What's on this leaf? Is it some kind of bug?"

She waited for him to pull his hand down and then he held his loose fist before her. "You actually caught a bug for me? Mr. Scared of Spiders has grown quite daring."

"It's not a spider. And don't tell anyone about the spider thing or there will be consequences." He jiggled his fist. "It's moving in there. Want to see what I caught?"

"Yes. Switzerland has some amazing insects…" She gaped when he opened his palm to reveal what should have flown off immediately. But it did not. In fact, it flashed and sparkled. "Are you kidding me?"

He took her hand and slid the ring he'd had concealed in his fist onto her finger. Then he dropped to one knee. "Ivy Quinn, you've shown me that love exists and that it is special and wondrous. You've won my heart and my trust. I don't know if there's a luckier man in the world. But I could get even luckier if you'd do me the honor of becoming my wife."

A warm summer breeze curled between them. Ivy's heart melted as she swallowed back tears. Bowing her head to his, she nodded. "Nothing would make me happier. I love you, Wolf. More than bugs."

"That's a hell of a lot. Take a closer look at the ring. I had it made special."

Ivy studied the ring. She was so excited she'd just seen a ring and her heart had started to race and—who cared if it was big—and then she saw the tiny pink butterfly at one end of a rose gold twist laden with diamonds. "Oh, my God, Wolf, this is…"

"I had it designed specially for you. Can't have you wearing a ring without a bug on it."

"It's perfect. Yes. Yes, I'll marry you!"

He sprang up and lifted her into his arms, spinning her. His shout attracted the interest of some from the nearby wedding party. And to them, he declared, "She said yes!"

* * * * *

*If you enjoyed this story,
check out these other great reads
from Michele Renae*

Parisian Escape with the Billionaire
The CEO and the Single Dad
Cinderella's Second Chance in Paris

All available now!